The Beautiful Dead Saga

Book 4

by

Daryl Banner

Published by Frozenfyre Publishing

Cover & Interior Design by Daryl Banner

Join Daryl's Mailing List!

Be the first to hear about his latest releases
and get an exclusive sneak peek behind the scenes
of being an author!

www.darylbanner.com/subscribe.html

Are you a member of Daryl's Doorway on Facebook?

It's a place to have fun, chat about everything
Daryl Banner, and hear the latest book-world news!
It's totally top secret, but here's the way in:

www.facebook.com/groups/darylsdoorway

The Beautiful Dead Saga

Book 1

The Beautiful Dead

Book 2

Dead Of Winter

Book 3

Almost Alive

Book 4

The Whispers

Book 5

Winter's Doom

Book 6

Deathless

List of Chapters

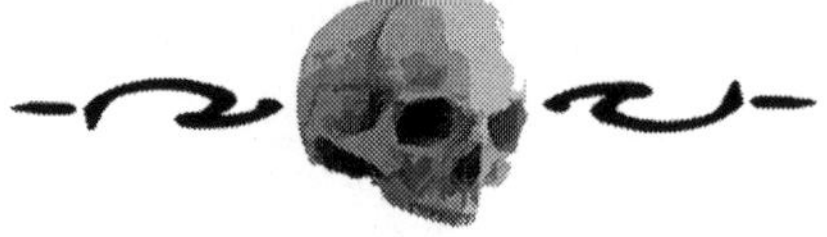

Prologue

"Blood."

I lift my head quickly. Bones snap in my neck that oughtn't. I grunt questioningly instead of using words; I stopped using words long ago.

"Blood," she repeats, pointing. "Smell."

Facing the dark and misty woods with my fingers and toes dug into the dry, cracked earth, I inhale deeply. It's not for need of oxygen; I'm welcoming in the scent of anything alive within about a billion mile radius. That's a deliberately gross exaggeration, of course, as time and distance mean nothing to the Dead.

I smell nothing. I hiss at her, annoyed.

She glares at me, her one eye glowing white through the mist and returning all my due annoyance. My sister's made of nothing but bones, loose skin, and attitude. A decrepit shred of colorless fabric that used to be a dress gives her approximately two helpings of modesty. She has no hair left on her head. I've forgotten if she's brunette like mom and I, or took after our redheaded dad. The colors blur in my memory. At a glance, it's tricky to tell which of us is the sister and which the brother, so similar in our near-skeletal figures we are.

"Blood," she insists stubbornly, then tears into the mist, swirls of grey coiling in her swift departure.

My knees snap loudly in protest as I chase her into the endless dark. Dead trees and white smoke whip past my face. That's all that fills my eyes: dead black trees, swirling white smoke. Colorlessness. There is no color in the world, none at all, except …

"Blood."

I find her at the foot of a fallen tree, its upturned roots tangled and thorny. Within its grasp there remains the bones of an animal. Deer, perhaps. Maybe a large dog. A horse. Elephant. Pigeon. What's the difference? Animals are all the same now. Just bones and teeth. Loose, decayed flesh, if lucky. And if really lucky, there's a speck of life left.

But not in this … carcass. I snort in frustration, my own little way of telling my sister she was wrong. So many false alarms. She looks up at me, her one white eye flashing with a storm of anger and sadness. *I know,* I'd say. *I'm disappointed too.* For a minute there, I believed her.

I wanted to believe her.

We move through the woods in silence, neither of us

looking at the other. We could go for years without saying a word. It's so rare to find blood anymore. Even a bird in the sky is a miracle, a fleeting and distant one. I'd plant my feet and twist my cracking neck to the sky just to watch as the free, Living little creature fluttered over the world. I'd give anything to be a bird …

If I wasn't so sure I'd eat myself.

"Blood," she whispers.

Not again. I huff furiously, shutting her up. There used to be twelve of us, but the others put themselves to sleep. That's what we call it, anyway. Maybe they'll wake back up if the sun ever rises. I doubt it's risen in a thousand years. Darkness and greyness and nothing is all that fills the hours of our endless days. Even sharing stories of our pasts has grown old. I know everything about my sister. She knows everything about me. There is nothing new to tell. Even words are dead.

My throat quivers, a hiss escaping my nostrils. My sister seems to hear because she sighs and says, "I know. I miss them too."

The others, maybe. Our parents. Our lives. I have no idea what she thinks I meant.

"Do you remember the one with the white hair?"

I scowl, annoyed somehow. I narrowly miss walking into a tree, distracted by her words. The mists begin to blind me. Everything looks the same. We can walk for hours and we're still in the same place. We can walk for years and never move and never sleep and never be free from the realm of the Dead.

"Winter white hair," she mutters at my side. "Funny. I can't even remember her face. It was so long ago."

I snort. I'm so tired of her stories. No matter the sun and the hope and the happiness they speak on and on about, it adds no sun to my days. Nothing ever will. The world is dead, and so's my sister's nauseating legends of mythic realms full of Livings and plants and water and … *life*. If such a place exists, I'd drain it of every last drop of blood. I would pin them to a tree just as I did the last clumsy heart-beating fool who dared to breathe the air of the Dead, who dared to walk the blight upon which our Dead feet tread, who dared to exist in our Dead, Dead, *Dead* realm. I'd give them one last look in their wet, quivery eyes before sinking my teeth into their delicious veins. I'd forget their face before they hit the ground.

The sound comes so suddenly, I mistake it for my sister's groaning at first. We look at one another, startled by the rumbling that stirs the mists.

"What's that?" she whispers.

My blank eyes are her answer.

Then, from above, we pay witness to the parting of the grey skies. Light flashes brightly, stunning us for a brief moment as the clouds are spread apart by a great metal bird. It roars loudly and shakes all the dead trees around us, as if jostling them to life. The metal bird moves fast, cutting through the mists above, roaring, growling, shaking the earth from its eternal rest.

It is not simply passing by; the great ugly beast is falling. It's so low that the tips of the dead trees crunch, shattering into great black splinters that rain upon the earth below, making way for the beast's descent. So low it goes that the trees begin to scream, cracking and snapping and breaking, brittle as bones. The metal beast thunders on through the distant mist beyond our view.

The sound is deafening. I haven't heard a thing that loud, Living or Dead, in a thousand years. That's yet another of my gross exaggerations.

Quite suddenly, the roaring stops and a ground-trembling boom tickles our bony feet. The great bird has landed. And not gently.

I stare at my sister, and her white eye glows with the same fear and fascination that flashes in mine.

We move through the mist in a hurry. The trees have bent and broken and fallen in the path of the beast. In a nest of shattered deadwood and dust, the metal thing rests in an eerie silence. Steam hisses from holes in its back, its own smoke swirling playfully from its wounds to dance with the mists of our Dead world.

"It opens," whispers my sister softly as a breath.

The belly of the capsized bird splits apart like a great metal door. From its bowels, three heads of healthy hair rise, their eyes squinting against the mist and the dark. The one in the middle, a handsome male with a chiseled jaw and brawny figure, lifts his wrist immediately, shining a fierce light upon his surroundings. Just behind him, a woman with more flesh in her cheeks than I've ever seen peers about, her large and colorful eyes searching the world in wonder.

But it's the third one who steals my attention, the one who actually appeared first. She turns her blushed and slender face to the left, then to the right. And she is terrified. Her wetted eyes reflect the fear I've come to recognize so well in any Living.

Then, despite the man's light never gracing the Dead flesh of my sister and I, the woman's keen eyes find mine in the dark. Her irises are bright and cold as ice, her hair white as winter.

The Living sees me. The Dead stare back.

That's when I hear the purring in my sister's throat, the sound of hunger that has been my song of days, our mantra, the Dead's one and only craving.

"Blood," I answer for the both of us—my first word in a million years—before we leap.

Chapter One

One Living Day Ago

"Oh, yes! The Dead live, my child! The Dead live!"

I softly tap my device, typing: *Crazy Lady Number Five. Her name is Dana. She smells like cat pee.*

"Oh, yes! I'm getting a real, real, real, real strong sense here." The bushy-haired woman in the silver robe rises, her veiny hands reaching up dramatically as if to snatch an imaginary bird from the air. Her big frog eyes blink once, two wet orbs shimmering, the irises grey as clay. "Oh!" she cries out. "Yes! YES! A really strong sense. Oh!" Her fingers wiggle in the air. "Yes! He's here! The spirit world has unraveled her scarf! She's unmasked her face! She's lifted her tricky veil!"

"The spirit world wears a lot of clothes," I remark.

Mercifully, she doesn't hear me. "When the spirit world speaks, the Living must listen to her!" she cries. "Oh! Your father has spoken, Jennifer! His name is Tom!"

I shake my head no.

"Terry?"

No.

"Tyson?"

Nope.

"Tin… Tim… T'uh… Starts with a T?"

No.

"P?"

Nope.

"D?"

Nopers.

"Z? Zane? Zimmy? Zoom?"

I offer an apologetic smile.

The woman gives a dramatic wave of her hand, her bushy hair trembling. "Oh, the spirit world is such a haze today, such a haze! The spirits must be shy …"

I tap more words into my device: *Dana is lonely. Her hair might be host to a family of pigeons.* My tummy groans. I wonder if my roommate Marianne will want to grab some breakfast before her first class.

"Your father, he enjoys … music?"

"No," I answer, considering if the bakery by the math building will be open this early in the morning.

"Glass art?"

"No."

"Your studies? Oh, he *loves* your studies, yes?"

"He thinks my studies are a joke."

"Oh. No, child." The woman's brow furrows. "There

is certainly nothing of a joke with the Dead. The Dead do not laugh. The Dead do not dream in humors."

"My studies aren't in the Dead," I reply patiently.

"Of course. You … You study the *Histories*." A pointy grin consumes her face. I worry no one's ever warned her of its effects; that smile could make children cry. "I adore the Histories. We will all be a part of it, someday. The Dead already are. And your father's spirit—"

"Is obviously not here," I finish for her.

"Oh, no! He is! He really is! He …" The woman looks up, searching for words, likely constructing the story in her head as she goes. Then her face flashes like she's just discovered the meaning to life. Well, that or the sun got in her eye. "He looks so handsome in his beige suit and … and his cream-colored tie! Oh, it's the cream of whipped vanilla bean, the stuff of clouds, of winter winds! Yes, I see it so clearly! He is here! He's just arrived!"

Really, it would be wise to treat her politely. This poor woman's sanity seems to be held on by a thread, and she hasn't had a visitor in weeks. I have to wonder where the hell *my* sanity was when I thought interviewing a diviner was a good idea. Her kind are mocked, labeled as weirdos, scaremongers, fanatics of tired myths of zombies roaming the planet making midnight snacks of our blood.

But maybe I'm a weirdo, too.

"This is going into your research, isn't it?" she asks

suddenly, the glow in her eyes replaced with something else entirely, something darker. "What you've seen here? The haze of the spirit world? The contact we've made? The will of the Dead? Do tell me."

I tap on my device: *She's hungry in the eyes. She does not see the spirit of my father; she only sees the dollar signs.*

"Yes," I answer.

"Seen and read and witnessed by h-h-hundreds?"

"Yes."

She nearly faints from the thought. I'm certain she imagines all of the business she will gain from the article I will write about her as part of my dissertation. Hundreds will read it. Thousands, maybe. Despite all the attention I've gotten for my important findings on the Histories of the second millennia, I know, however, that the masses are only truly interested in the one tiny section of my studies. The section titled: *The Beautiful Dead.*

Maybe they all think I'm a fool, too. Maybe they are hungrily awaiting my words, just like this woman is, so they can laugh at me. The girl with the ridiculous dream. The girl who believes in tales told among children under their bed sheets to give one another a scare. The girl who believes that a society of Living Dead once existed.

"W-Where are you going?"

I'm at the door. "Thank you for your time, Dana."

"B-But … But I haven't even gazed into my crystal

ball! Or, or, or turned over a card or two to surmise your future! Or given you a most significant message sent to me through the haze!—a message from your father!"

I close my device and pocket it, then lend the poor lady a look of disappointment. "I wanted to believe, Dana. Dana the Diviner ..."

"You *are* a believer!" she sings. "You believe in the Living Dead, yes! The Precious Dead!"

"The Beautiful Dead," I agree. "They, I believe in with all my soul. And I so wanted to believe you too, but my father cannot possibly send me a message from the spirit world, because my father is still alive."

An unfortunate twitch suddenly occupies her left eye.

"You ..." Her heart breaks before my eyes. "Y-You ... You tricked me ...?"

"Good day, Dana."

The door is shut and I'm halfway down the road when I hear her call after me, crying out my name and cursing me for my deception. Yes, I deceived her, but with a good intention: I *so* wanted her to prove me wrong. I wanted her to know the truth through the haze of the "spirit world" she claimed to see. I wanted to believe, but ...

"You evil little girl!" she screams.

It is the last thing I hear before turning the corner, her voice diffused to nothing but a vague noise at my back.

The shuttle arrives right on time, taking me up the

long polished metal road lined with pretty houses toward the university, which looms with its tall spires and buildings that shine like long glass fingers in the angry glow of the rising sun.

At this early hour, I don't imagine my roommate will be up, so I make a detour to the bakery near the math building to pick up a few fresh helpings for breakfast. The woman there is always sweet to me and asks about my progress in class, but today she is more subdued. Perhaps she senses my ire from the recent disappointment. I am not skilled at preventing inner emotions from warring across my face, regrettably. That's a talent in which my roommate is a notable expert.

When I open the door to my campus condominium, the floor-to-ceiling glass window shows a breathtaking portraiture of the university burned orange and gold with the brilliant beams of the sun. To that magnificence, I huff and sourly gnash my finger into a button on the wall. Metal blinds flip shut, casting the room into darkness. I throw my coat over the couch, then drop the baked goods on the end table, certain the scent of them will rouse my sleeping roommate. Her door is closed and no light glows from underneath it. I pluck a croissant from the bag to answer the growing cry from my belly, then move slowly across the den to my bedroom. I open the door gently.

Lying on the bed is my secret roommate who we

pretend does not live here. His name is John. We're sort of lovers and sort of friends. It's complicated. It's against some rule that he, a non-student, lives here in a campus-issued condominium, but he's yet to be caught because I'm smart and my roommate, loyal. Watching him sleep brings me a strange and relieving sense of joy. I can't explain it other than to state the obvious: he's beautiful when he sleeps. For all his brawn and ruggedness, he appears so innocent and gentle lying there in my bed cuddling one of my pillows and breathing softly.

But if I'm completely honest with myself, our little … *arrangement*, should I call it? … does not come without its due doubts. Is John just using me? Sure, he cleans the place up while I'm in class and sometimes he'll even cook a meal in our kitchen for all of us (using the ingredients that *I* buy, no less), but is he only playing nice because we haven't reported him to the university? Am I just a means by which he can stay close to the school that he so desperately wants to attend? If he ever gains acceptance to the Engineering program and the financial aid decide that he's worthy enough to assist, will he simply go, leaving me in the dust of his dreams? Though Marianne is too polite to say so, I know the doubt has crossed both our minds. *He's just for now*, I worry and fear most nights. *He's biding his time. He's tolerating you. He doesn't love you.*

Then again, when John draws his warm, beefy body

against mine in the night and I feel his strong arms wrap tight around me, a thrill chases its way through my stomach and up my throat, stealing all of my breath. My heart dances and a stupid smile breaks across my face.

Maybe I should rather be asking: am *I* using *him?*

My whole room smells like him now. I don't mind at all. We share things. One time, we revisited the gardens, my favorite place on campus. The day John and I met, we sorta kinda stole a tiny insignificant rock from the gardens that was encased in special glass. The ugly thing now sits on my nightstand and watches over me as I sleep. It may look dull on the outside, but that rock carries within it a deep, precious sentiment.

Maybe someday, I won't have to doubt that he's just here for now. Maybe someday, John will say he loves me.

"Jen?"

I turn. Marianne is standing at her door, now open. Her puffy cheeks are glowing red. *Literally*. It's a fashion trend that I'm not particularly taken by, but Marianne is, and she now has a vast collection of glow-in-the-dark makeup that she proudly wears, making her cheeks look like two enormous demon's eyes that jiggle as she speaks.

"Marianne," I whisper, stepping back out of my room and quietly shutting the door so as not to disturb John. "I brought croissants. Help yourself."

"Oh, okay." She stares at them, not helping herself.

I study her for a moment. "Something wrong?"

Before she answers, the device in my pocket vibrates with alarm. I pull it out and look at the new message.

"Oh, crap." I toss the last bite of bread onto the table. "Professor. I'm being called to his office. The deadline for my dissertation is fast approaching. Algebra final's coming up too, and I have this dumb essay I have to write for my Archaic Languages class. I wish the only thing I had to worry about was my Histories dissertation. Really, the school expects us undergrads to study so much all at once, while all we want to do is follow our *main* studies, and—" I look up at my roommate. "Sorry, I'm rambling. Are you okay? Did you want to tell me something?"

She takes my last bite and crams it into her mouth with the deftness of an assassin. The chewing movement of her glowing red cheeks combined with a queer look in her eye is all the answer I'll get, apparently.

"I'll be back in an hour."

I don my black coat once again, then quickly check the condition of my face in the long mirror by the door. My white-blonde hair runs in tragic tangles to my waist, and my pale, slender face looks as if I haven't touched a full meal in days. *I am the Living Dead*, I jest to myself.

"Need a little touch?" Marianne offers sympathetically. "Some eyes? A color for your cheeks, maybe?"

"Desperately as I wish to have mine glowing like pink

light bulbs for my professor, I'll pass." I blow Mari a kiss. "If John wakes before I'm back, tell him the diviner was a total fake. It'll crush him, but he was eager to know."

"Oh … That's too bad. I'd hoped she was real."

Me too, I might say, but instead I just give Mari a little wink before slipping out the door.

The morning air is as crisp as I'd left it just a moment ago. I move across campus with a swiftness, passing the Floating Fountain on the way, as well as the Trim Tree, which is visible from the window of my condominium. The Courtyard of Steel makes a tap with my every step as I cross it on my way to the Histories building where, at its topmost spire, Professor Praun awaits.

To stand in the presence of Professor Praun is to know whether one's wobbly knees can actually support one's weight. Though many are intimidated by his mere presence, others tremble at his reputation for keeping a strict classroom and stricter grade book. Perpetually foul of eye and mood, the man wears a razor-sharp black goatee dusted lightly with silver. That's the only bit of hair on his smooth, dark head. Even his eyebrows are shaven; strange as it looks, it's a unique style they used to take on when he himself was a student.

"Jennifer," he says, his cool voice ringing across the unnecessarily enormous and reverberant office he keeps.

"Professor." I stop halfway across the room, unable to

bear the sound of my footsteps echoing loudly.

He's facing away from me, staring out of the glass wall that forms the north side of his office, his hands clasped behind his back. With the glow of the sun on his skin, in this moment he appears godly.

"You came to me as a Theories major," he states.

I swallow once. "Yes, professor."

"Specialized in History and Mythology."

"Yes. Right."

"As a studier of Mythology, you further specialized in the … Undead."

Just that tiny pause in his sentence pours a cold and discomforting stream of anxiety down my body. It does not matter the progress I've made in my time here nor how much of a grown woman I think I've become; in this instant, I'm an unlearned child with noodles for knees.

He turns finally, gracing me with his cold, stern eyes, the whites flashing brightly in contrast with his dark skin.

"Tell me, Jennifer. What first inspired you to abandon your course of study and shift to a pure Histories major?"

Unable to meet his eyes, I address the general vicinity of his throat when I answer. "I found it fascinating."

"And you felt that a wise decision?"

Obviously it wasn't, as is evidenced by this meeting. Of course, that's not what I answer. Still staring at his throat, I say, "I … felt at the time that I connected more with …

with studies of our past … and—"

"Your dissertation is due in just one week's time." He takes a few steps in my direction, coming around the front of his desk. "There is quite a stirring in the conversations of my students. I may speak all day in auditoriums, but I listen twice as well. That's why we're born with two ears and one mouth."

"A stirring in conversations of your students?" I echo, afraid to connect the dots.

"Everyone is so very, very, *very* curious about … one particular part of your dissertation."

"I know," I say at once, caving, trembling, suffocating. Is there any air in this room at all? "I know what you said. I remember every word of our conversation, but I—"

"Come."

He moves across the office, drawing close to a round table upon which a holograph of our planet floats lazily. I stand on the other side of the table. Sweat has gathered under my arms. My throat is clenching shut, as if refusing me the right to breathe.

"Here," he says, pointing at the holograph. It shows the planet glimmering in hues of green and gold. "See?"

I nod wordlessly.

"Our university, right by the ocean, edge of the world. Look at our forests. Look at Crystal River, see it?"

I nod again, staring listlessly at the professor's jacket

visible through the flickering holographic image.

"We have water. We have food in ample supply, and we mind the recycling of our resources. We are a diligent, self-sustaining society. Do you know who wasn't?"

Obviously. Everyone does. It's half my dissertation.

"*Them,*" he mutters, spinning the holograph of the planet around with one dramatic wave of his hand. In striking contrast, the other side of the world is dark and colorless, its landmasses appearing like giant blots of ink and ruin, its oceans a sickening, mottled purple.

I would never dream of disrespecting Professor Praun, but how can he call into question all of my work when I haven't even yet presented it to him? "Please, professor," I begin to beg. "I know what they're all saying, but I—"

"It's an embarrassment to the Histories department," he declares, each of his words like an icicle into my chest; I feel their effect in my fingertips. "Nothing can survive there, living *or* dead. It's a ruined realm beyond the sun's reach, nothing more. It's a reminder of our past mistakes, and how greedy our ancestors were. Nothing. More."

"The Sunless Reach," I recite. "They call it the Sunless Reach, where the Dead live and the Living die, and—"

"Your Beautiful Dead do not exist."

I swallow hard. I feel the hint of tears grace my eyes, which frustrates me to no end, how my face betrays me. The last thing I want is for Professor Praun to witness me cry; he wouldn't spare an inch of sympathy for me.

"I warned you, Jennifer Steel."

I can't meet his eyes, nor speak. I'm struggling to keep all the tears in my face and not allow a single one to spill.

"I warned you when you began your dissertation. I witnessed the embarrassment of your first presentation at the start of last term, and when you shifted your studies to the Histories, I *warned* you to tread lightly in my department, yet your arrogance persists."

Staring at the holographic world—one half alive, one half not—I manage one last plea: "P-Professor ..."

He steps close, too close. "If you print a *word* about your so-named Beautiful Dead, you will be expelled from Skymark University. If I so much as *hear* a word like 'Undead' uttered from your lips, I will personally escort you off the campus myself. Am I made clear, Ms. Steel?"

Unable to speak, I nod once.

Professor Praun studies me a while, perhaps waiting for me to humiliate myself further with a spilling of tears and snot and grossness from my indignant face. Then, unexpectedly, he puts a hand on either of my shoulders and lowers his chin, eyeing me directly.

In a calm, softer voice, he says, "You are an intelligent young woman. You are capable of great things, Jennifer. You have excellent grades. Please, don't let your potential go to waste. Focus your dissertation on the *survival* of the

Living, and what we've *learned* from our Histories. Do not waste it on the Dead. The Dead do *not* live. That is why we bury them, so that they may rest for all of eternity."

His gentle, well-meaning words sting me worse than a condescending pat on the head. It does nothing to ward away the tears that still threaten to spill, nor does it do a thing to help my ever-clenching nerves.

"I look forward to your presentation next week." He drops his hands from my shoulders. "Good day."

The walk back home is slow and frigid. Surprisingly, the tears never spill. As the sun now paints the campus in a zillion shades of gold, my mind fights with every last word that my professor uttered. No matter how furious I am, I know I have no recourse. Why did he pick *now* to put an end to my dreams? What harm was my innocent studying going to cause? Was he afraid of waking the Dead … which he doesn't believe in, anyway? Is he secretly scared of ghosts? Did he just lose a loved one and resents my interest in the subject? Why do books exist on the Living Dead if we weren't meant to believe them?

I only make it halfway back to the condominium before dropping onto a bench at the edge of the campus, suffering with the weight of my professor's disapproval. I hug myself and stare into the sky and the fire that now bleeds across it. My attention is caught by a hovercraft floating through the field of trees beyond the perimeter of campus. I wonder for a while what it's doing there, resorting to making up hilarious reasons for its existence. *It is transporting more oxygen from the forest to us, the Living,* I decide. The hum of the machine soothes me somehow, and I find myself closing my eyes, seduced into a state of half-sleep. Waking up so early to visit Dana the Diviner certainly did a number to my sleep schedule. I feel myself tilting back, my head threatening to float me into a realm of dreams if I'm not careful.

A gust of wind rouses me, and I open my eyes just in time to witness the hovercraft soar high above my head on its trek over the campus. I stare after it for a while, watching as it disappears, taking with it the gentle hum I was so enjoying. And there goes my peace.

"He didn't even give me a decent reason," I complain to Marianne when I meet her and John at the dormitory cafeteria for an early lunch. "Just a general 'Stop or else!' sort of spiel."

"So awful. And after all your inquiries and books and things," agrees Marianne sympathetically, forking a bite of sugared fruit past her lips.

John shakes his head. "He can't just do that."

"He did." I sip on my mint-and-water.

"No." John folds his muscular arms, tensing up in that way that pops out a vein or two in his forehead. He turns his handsome face, his lips pursed in frustration, which shows off his stubble and chiseled jawline. "You have a right to study whatever you want," he says, brooding. "That's the whole damn purpose of the university … of education. *I* think for myself. I'm innovative. What the hell do I have to do to prove myself to the university? To earn the damn financial aid? I *know* I'm better than half their Engineering students. They have no new ideas."

I study the side of his fuming face, that nagging worry chasing its way into my chest again. Is it really all about John? As soon as the university *does* accept him, is he out of my life forever?

"At least you have a place to stay," I point out, then realize how badly I sound like I'm fishing for gratitude. "And a salad," I add quietly, my eyes dropping to the tasty one that sits on the table before him.

He regards it with a smirk, then channels all his fury at the university into that salad, as if its innocent greens and berries were now to blame.

"I told you, you could sneak into my biology classes," says Marianne with a shrug. "My professor doesn't know any of our names or faces. I don't even know if she knows her own. She wears blouses backwards sometimes. I don't think it's intentional. You'd be perfectly hidden."

John rolls his eyes irritably. "Thanks, but I haven't yet grown a fondness for Anatomy or Biology or Blood."

"I love Blood," she whispers while sucking the dear

life out of an innocent strawberry.

I take John's hand. He seems startled by the action at first, as if a spider had just leapt upon his fingers. "We will sort out this ridiculous situation with your acceptance and with the financial aid, John. We'll write a letter showing all your accomplishments and Engineering knowhow and your … your hunger for more. It'll be a dissertation of your own," I insist. "We'll change their minds."

"As certainly as you'll change Praun's," agrees John with acid sarcasm, then pulls his hand from mine.

I frown, annoyed by his reaction. Does he think of me at all? Does it occur to him how much I've done for him? "I'm trying to help, John. I know you're upset, but—"

"What I mean is, I'm not allowed to be a student," he goes on bitterly, "and you can't study what you *want* to study because your professor finds it embarrassing. I think the concept of the Beautiful Dead is so … *brilliant*. Who does this school serve? Its brilliant students, or itself?"

I wonder for a second if John just called me brilliant, or if it was just a passing, general remark. With a sigh, I set down my spoon, creating a metal bridge from one side of my noodle-and-berry soup to the other, then express my complete and utter surrender to Praun's philosophy. "You know, I think my professor … has a point."

Marianne and John face me as one, surprised.

"After all," I continue, "no one has ever *seen* the Dead.

Seeing is believing, is it not? The Sunless Reach is only half an ocean *that* way," I say, pointing. "There's no evidence of their existence. None. After all these years, why have we seen nothing of their kind here on our side of the planet? Don't they ... thirst? What sustains them? Wouldn't they smell our blood half a world away and swim across the ocean to feast on us?" I look at either of my friends, beseeching them. "Doesn't it make sense? Professor Praun's doubts are not unfounded. In fact ... maybe, if I were to be honest, I ... I share his doubts."

"This is about the dumb diviner," says John.

I wrinkle my face. "What? No. I just meant—"

"She turned out to be a fake, just like the last four crazy fanatics you met with, and now you're discouraged and calling it quits." John leans across the table, his face drawing close to mine. "The Jennifer I know doesn't quit. She fights. Her heart still beats."

The Jennifer he knows ...? My heart still beats. Does John really know me at all? Maybe I'm the one who's holding back. Maybe *he's* waiting for *me* to open up.

I turn my head, pulled by the deep purring of an engine just outside the cafeteria. Though I know it's likely my imagination, the engine sends a vibration through the whole room. I feel the vibrations in my fingers, in my toes, in my eyelashes ...

In my heart ... which still beats, but now quicker.

A poet in my Theories class last semester once spoke bravely about the human necessity for passions and wiles and recklessness. Isn't there such a thing as well-intended deception? As an honest thief? As a lie told … in order to reach a most valuable truth?

"John, Marianne." I smile innocently. "What are your plans today?"

Mari squints suspiciously at me. John's brow narrows.

"Follow me … if you want to make History."

As swiftly as a thought, I dash out of the cafeteria. Down the hall I go until I reach the back door which, upon opening, spills the light of impending noon over my face. I skirt around the edge of the building until I'm upon the very large object of my desire.

I don't need to turn around to know John and Mari are on my heels waiting and, if they're smart, *worried* on what I have spontaneously planned to do.

"We have to make a run for it when the pilot debarks the craft with his delivery crew," I tell them. "We're not going to have much time."

"What??" protests John. "No way …"

"My heart's still beating," I note. "Isn't yours?"

"Racing," John verifies. "When I said the Jennifer I know fights, stealing food from a university hovercraft isn't what I meant."

"We're not stealing the food," I tell him. "We're

stealing the craft."

That answer inspires an audible rasp from poor Mari. "No!" she exclaims in a hushed whisper. "We're *not* doing that! No, no, no. I'm with John on this. What in Dead hell are you planning to do with a *hovercraft??*"

I face my friends, the worried pair of them. "Professor Praun also told me I was an intelligent young woman. He told me not to waste my potential. So here I am, *not* wasting my potential." I smirk at my cleverness. "Praun told me the Beautiful Dead don't exist. I'm going to prove him wrong. And when I return with my proof, it won't be their laughs I earn anymore." I face the craft once again, determined. "I know they're out there. I'm going to the Sunless Reach, whether with or without you two."

"With," decides John suddenly.

I'd hoped he'd say that. I study the side of his face, curious what made him suddenly change his mind. Is he going to say it now? Is he going to tell me how much he cares about me? Is he going to say that it's his undying love and admiration for me that inspires his courage?

"If I have any part in you making the world's greatest Historic discovery of our time," he says, "imagine what the financial aid would say. The Engineering department. They'll *have* to accept me then. I won't have to hide."

Well, I should've expected that angle. "John ..."

"No." He cuts me off, stubbornly shaking his head.

"I'm coming with you. You can't possibly do something this radically irresponsible alone."

He wants to be close to me. I want to believe that this handsome person I invited into my home and broke rules for actually has deeper feelings for me. Feelings that go beyond the kisses, beyond the cuddling at night, beyond the brooding demeanor he wears on the outside. Surely, beneath that body of stone, therein lies a heart that beats as hungrily as mine.

"They could imprison us for theft," I point out.

"We could go the rest of our lives believing the lie they feed us," John says back, "that the Dead never lived. Ever since the day I met you, Jennifer, I've believed you. I want to see it for myself."

Marianne, in a rare moment of defiance, stands in front of me like a round wall of fabric, dramatic hair, and over-rouged cheeks. "I'm not letting you do this, Jen. I've been with you since we took that class together our first year. I've seen you act irrationally and I've picked you up every time your crazy decisions have shattered you. Jen, you're throwing away your future if you do this."

"I'm throwing it away if I don't," I retort.

The bottom of the hovercraft opens with a harsh, metallic groan. The ramp slides out and touches the ground, giving a path for the pilot to exit, followed by four men who each carry a smooth metal crate. In a matter of seconds, they're out of sight and the hovercraft waits like a great and patient creature.

"Now's our chance," I whisper. "Mari, I love you. Please water my Hydra's Kiss twice a week for me until I'm back."

"I don't even know what that is," Mari complains.

"I'll see you again when I'm back with proof of the Beautiful Dead."

With that, I slip around Mari, who makes no effort to stop me, and hurry for the ramp. For as close as it is, just the crossing of the courtyard seems to take ages. I feel every eye of the world on me, imaginary or not, as if the authorities are already alerted to my brash, criminal act. I can already hear my mom and dad admonishing me for my foolishness. *Don't worry,* I imagine myself explaining to all of them. *I'm only borrowing the school's property, and it's for a very good cause.* I'm sure they'll be understanding.

I've never been aboard a hovercraft before. The sound of my shoes against the metal is softer than expected, and it smells clean as polished silver with a hint of something medicinal, like an antiseptic bandage or a hospital room. My lungs fill with the cool, sterile air as I enter the craft, surprised to find so many crates and undelivered parcels still aboard. *That means the crew will be back soon for another trip,* I realize. We'll have to act fast.

The craft itself is quite small, approximately the length

of my bedroom inside, an oblong oval lined with chrome plates, blinking screens with numbers and lights flashing across them, and a thin neon blue strip of light that runs down its center, terminating at an expansive control panel in the front.

I walk toward the controls, daunted by them. The sun burns bright through the front windshield, blinding me. It is a very annoying and inconvenient time to be almost-noon. I shield my eyes, trying to understand the console.

"Can you fly this thing?" asks John at my side.

I imagine racing the hovercraft across the gardens, cutting every tree in half. I imagine colliding into the math building, killing us all in one fell explosion. I imagine flipping the craft over with its own hover propulsion technology, ending us all on our heads or worse.

"Can't be too hard," I answer instead, trembling.

Marianne, to my surprise, emerges by my other side. "Please, Jen. Please reconsider. We can speak to the president of the school. Maybe she could reach some sort of compromise with your professor and, like, publish your findings under Myths instead of Histories. Wouldn't that be a reasonable compromise?"

"Publish it as fiction instead of fact, you mean?" I try and fail to hide the resentful tone in my voice.

"Your mother would be so disappointed in you, Jen." Mari's trying to hit me where it hurts; at the mention of my mother, however, it *does* hurt. "What happens when they find out you've stolen a craft? They'll locate you. I'm certain they can. They'll, like, override the controls or something. You won't even make it to the water—they won't let you." Mari puts a hand on mine, and now she knows how terribly I tremble; she literally *feels* my doubt. "It isn't too late. We can just go. You and I, we'll go and request a meeting with the president. She will see you. You're top in your department. Professor Praun will appreciate your initiative, if nothing else."

With my resolve suddenly broken, I abandon the confusing mess of buttons and dials and knobs, turning my sullen face to John, my final appeal, my dwindling light. I see the truth in his eyes: I've lost my mind.

"Jen," my roommate goes on to my back. "There's … something I didn't tell you. This morning when John was asleep and you came home. I … I couldn't tell you."

I look at Mari, her glowing red cheeks dancing as she speaks, her bright purple irises shining with sympathy as her gaze meets mine.

"Your mother called on the holograph," says Mari. Her mouth opens, then closes, then opens to say, "She … She had news, Jennifer."

"News …?"

Marianne swallows hard. Then, tears fill her eyes before words can fill her mouth. And in that instant, somehow, I already know what she can't say.

"My father," I whisper.

"L-Late last n-night," Mari confirms, the tears letting go. "Oh, Jen, I'm so sorry! He went to sleep and never woke! Oh, Jen! His heart stopped … His heart stopped!" Her puffy hands slap over her mouth, the tears dressing them as she shudders with emotion.

I stare at her, struck by the news. I'm about to shout at her, asking why the hell she didn't tell me earlier, but suddenly the whole world becomes Marianne's two sad, purple eyes, and I can't say anything at all. In the swirling numb nothingness that's become of my mind, I suddenly find myself struggling to remember the last time my father and I spoke. What did we talk about? Was it something as trivial and silly as the weather, or some gripe I had with the workload of a class, or a thing I read in the paper? When was the last time I said I love him?

"Your mother is going to need you," says Mari after a wet and particularly demonstrative sniffle. "Let's go home and give her a call, alright?"

I picture him standing in front of me. I picture him in a beige suit and cream-colored tie, the cream of whipped vanilla bean … the stuff of clouds, of winter winds. I could almost laugh. The last thing he'd want is for me to run back home to mother, casting away my dreams when I've come this close. He might've thought little of my studies, but he thought much of me. Maybe I'm just trapped in my little tornado of insanity, caught up in a moment of reckless passion, but he would want me to do this. I know it. Isn't it strange? To have received such terrible news, and yet oddly have been in the perfect state in which to receive it? It's almost like I don't believe her, like I don't believe he's dead. How could a person like me believe in true death, anyway? There's more than one kind of dying. There's more than one kind of Dead.

"Why are you smiling?"

I look Mari in the eyes. "It's a sign," I tell her.

"Yes?" she encourages me, eager to go home.

I nod cheerfully, then face the console and stab the red button with my finger.

The ramp slams shut with a guttural bang that sends a rattle through our bones and inspires a shriek from Mari. I press my hand to the central touchscreen and push hard. The craft leans forward suddenly, screeching in the effort, and amidst a scream of terror from Mari, we launch into the air the height of a building, then soar onward.

"STOP!"

The unfamiliar voice startles me, and I spin to face it. From an unseen compartment which may or may not have been the bathroom, a uniformed young man who couldn't be more than eighteen years old spills onto the deck with his pants down. He wears a formfitting white shirt embroidered at the breast with the company logo. His pants, which he scrambles to pull back up, are pleated and starched, and he has slippers for shoes. A tiny white cap sits loosely on his head of bright blonde hair, neither of which hide his fast-growing eyes. They grow bigger when he seems to realize we're airborne, and his gloved hands raise up. It doesn't occur to me why he has them raised until John mutters, "He thinks we're robbing him."

"WHO'RE YOU!?" the uniformed boy asks, or rather, screams.

"Your new pilots!" I answer cheerfully, then return my gaze to the front just in time to see the face of the Histories building plunging towards us.

"JENNIFER!"

A panicked shift of my palm on the touchscreen twists the craft into a full-blown barrel-roll, skirting the edge of the building and thrusting us over the spire of another. Thrown off my feet, I fly back, tumbling past the panicked boy whose screams join that of my roommate's.

"John!" I cry out, spotting him at the front gripping a chair, his muscles bulging from the effort. "The controls!"

He slaps a hand to the touchscreen where mine was, then struggles to keep the craft balanced, though not well. The whole ship lurches left, swings right, then seems to balance itself. My body is so disoriented suddenly, I can't tell if we're ascending or descending, if we're turning left or right or nowhere at all.

The uniformed boy collapses near me, his cap flying off his head, and he clutches a nearby tied-down crate the way a child grips his pillow during a nightmare. I'm that nightmare; *I* just happened to his day. His quivering blue eyes find mine. An ugly gash now decorates his forehead, appearing like a long and red third eyebrow. He seems to be muttering to himself, perhaps praying to some god or goddess I studied once in my Mythologies.

Carefully rising to my feet and grabbing hold of a steel beam for balance, I ask him, "Can you fly?"

"I'm in training!" he cries out miserably. "Today is my first day! I have math class in forty minutes! What the hell are you guys doing??"

"You've trained, though?" I encourage him hopefully. "You've had, um ... simulations and ... and practice, yes?"

"I'm a d-d-d-delivery boy!" he shouts, hardly able to even deliver his words. "Put the craft down! Now! I'll tell the authorities if you don't! You'll be expelled! You'll—"

"Well," I say, cutting him off and trying unsuccessfully to steel my own shaken nerves. "If we can manage to find a spot, delivery boy, then we'd be happy to land and let you out. Really, it's a total accident you're here. There's no sense in you coming with us if—"

"We can't," calls John from the front.

I look ahead, watching the buildings and spires fling

past us, the ship hurtling ceaselessly towards the edge of campus. "Why not?"

"They've been notified," he says. "Authorities, I see them." The view shifts leftwards, rightwards, upwards. My guts somersault, somehow unable to register the erratic movement. "If we turn back now, we face certain, harsh criminal charges. Prison for life. I can't even think. We'll be branded thieves, Jennifer. Endangering lives. It's too … It's too late to turn back," he says and realizes, perhaps not having truly considered the consequence of his committing to my insanity until just now.

I look at Marianne from across the cabin, surveying her as she desperately clings to the copilot's chair and stares back at me, a look of utter loss in her colorful eyes.

"I'm so sorry," I say, unsure if my words can be heard.

Mari hears them. She gives a wistful shrug, then says, "Hell … I can't remember … the last time … I had … this much fun …"

"I'm not having fun," the uniformed boy lets us know, still clinging to the crate with all his precious life. "You're all criminals. I shouldn't be here! Let me off! NOW!"

"Can't," I say sadly. "You're coming on the fieldtrip of a lifetime, apparently. Hope you remembered to get your permission slip signed by a parent or legal guardian."

"Fieldtrip to where??" he asks miserably.

Through the front glass, I watch as the campus flashes

out of view, and all that sprawls out ahead of us is sand, the ocean looming ahead like endless blue silk. The boy's question goes unanswered. The fear of what we've done washes over all of us, just as certainly as the blue of the ocean meets our eyes and the world of the Living falls to our backs. The silence between us speaks the worth of a thousand crippling words.

I wonder if we're all thinking the same thing. Our faith is certainly being tested now. Is the other side of the world *really* depleted of all life, ruined and decayed from the centuries? Does the Sunless Reach even exist, or is it all ocean out there? Is it truly … *the realm of the Dead?*

If time were an endless plain, the ocean is the chasm cut deep in the earth, its watery yawn spanning far beyond what light can reach. This awesome rift, we will never know for sure how wide it is. But on the other side, as sure as we are that there *is* another side, that's where our story truly begins. Not where the land ends, but far, far beyond its lazy shores … in a realm beyond the sun's reach, where the Dead live and the Living …

… the Living …

"Are you okay, Jennifer?"

I turn at the sound of John's voice. *My father would have wanted this,* I tell myself again, desperate to believe the words I'm forcing through my mind, now invaded by a tiny doubt that wasn't there before.

The crazy lady Dana summoned his spirit from the world beyond, remember? He's here with you, wearing that silly beige suit. It doesn't matter what your last words were to him.

Honor him in the only way you can …

"When we return with our proof," I answer, "we will be celebrated. The president will honor us. You know, my dad always used to ask me, 'What did you do today?' The question never before held such weight. This day, my friends … This day, we write *our* chapter in the Histories." I face my roomie. "Mari, you'll be revered for your new findings in Biology and Human Anatomy and Blood. The Living Dead, Marianne! You will know them as certain as you know the colors of your cheeks and eyes. They will talk about your discoveries for years to come …"

"I've forgotten which color I put in today," Mari moans, bringing a sorrowful hand to her face, mourning the lack of a mirror.

"We're the new History," I declare, happy with my dream. "Isn't that a worthwhile way to spend your day?"

"Yes," agrees John, "given we survive the journey."

The four of us stare ahead, a view of the ageless ocean meeting our eager, dreaming eyes with its silent eternity of unknowable depths and greedily-kept secrets.

Chapter Two

The Lightless Realm

I wake to the shriek of an alarm.

"John! What's happening?!" Marianne cries out.

"I don't know, I don't know. We were cruising just fine, but then—"

"The window is clouding up!"

"Anti-fog!" shouts the delivery boy. "Turn on the—"

"What is this stupid indicator indicating?? Everything's blinking! Make it stop!"

I stagger to my feet, bracing myself against the wall. The only thing in view is still endless ocean and nothing. I have no idea how long I was asleep, how much time has passed, how far we've traveled …

"We're losing altitude," reports John, inspecting dials and poking buttons.

"I don't want to drown," the delivery boy mutters to himself, eyes glued to the pilot's console with a look of utter loss. "It's a horrible way to go."

"At this rate, we'll explode before we drown," mutters

John with a grunt. "See? Bright side to everything."

"NOW'S NOT A TIME FOR JOKES!" shrieks the boy.

The alarm keeps spitting digital bullets into our ears, flooding the cabin with aural panic. Marianne sucks at her fingers and tosses fruitless suggestions on what to do, to which John irritably explains that they're not plummeting into the ocean; we're merely descending at a miniscule rate. Something's clearly wrong—hence the alarm—but he wouldn't have a first clue of what. The delivery boy wonders aloud if the craft might float in water. "Just what we need," moans Mari miserably, "to turn our adventure into a lost-at-sea nightmare."

"Land."

The three of them turn to me, their arguing ceased. Mari and the boy are confused while John stares at me, brooding with dark resolve.

"Land," I repeat, hurrying to the front and pointing at the foggy glass.

The others look. With the farthest reach of our eyes, we see a strip of darkness so thin we're likely all doubting it's even there—a mere illusion, this thread of shadow stitching together the distant horizon and sea. Watching in utter silence, we hold our breath as the hovercraft floats across the air, the ocean rushing past us beneath our toes. Is the shadow growing closer? Is it real?

Mari whispers, "It looks ..."

"Ugly," finishes the boy in fear.

"Mysterious," agrees Mari.

With the crawl of each second that passes, the needle of darkness that separates water and sky begins to grow tiny stems that almost don't exist. The tiny, tiny stems grow sluggishly taller, taller, taller … until they become the smallest skeletons of dead, leafless trees I've ever seen. What at first looks to be an innocent cloud soon reveals itself as a thick, wooly blanket of mist that sleeps atop the trees. This mist doesn't stir or move or swirl. Neither do the trees seem to sway. It looks like a painting against the sky. The thorny terrain grows and grows until it becomes something as promised and imminent as death itself.

John rushes to the controls, gently pressing his palm to the touchscreen while the alarm incessantly barks. He pokes about the console, searching for something.

"He doesn't know how to land the craft," the delivery boy realizes in horror. "We're going to crash!"

"Of *course* I don't know how to land the damn thing. Do I look like a pilot to you?" John growls at him, his ire causing his hand to flinch, which in turn causes the craft to twitch. He literally holds the vehicle in the palm of his hand—and all of us with it. "If I can't get it to slow down, I'm going to guide us to a plain or flatland of some sort. If we crash, we're going to crash *gently*, damn it."

Land rushes towards us much quicker now. In stark

contrast to our own beach, the sands here look so grey, it's like they've had their color extracted somehow. The shore comes closer and closer and closer. The mists …

"I can't see anything," John realizes, and the fear in his voice does nothing to reassure the rest of us. "That thick fog, I can't see through it. I can't see where we're landing. *I can't see anything!"*

Before we can count the fingers on our hands, the shore is behind us and yet another vast blanket lies in all directions, except this blanket is made of an unmoving, opaque, grey-white haze. I daresay the view inspires far more fear and mystery than the ocean did.

I'm at John's side. "You can do it," I cheer him on. "Maybe you can pull back against the oncoming wind to slow us down," I suggest, "like this."

I put my hand on his. The touch of our skin breaks the tension in his face, if just a little, and his lips part. I move my fingers to guide his. Isn't it strange, that even in a time like this when our lives literally hang in the balance, I find myself longing for his attention? Why do John and I have to play this game? I get no thrill in the chase. It makes my stomach writhe, worrying and recalling every single time my heart's been broken or neglected or betrayed. Can't we just say what we feel and *know* the relationship we have? Or does he *enjoy* the endless, emotional mystery?

"We can use the wind," I whisper calmly. "Then, the

moment we break through the mist …"

The ruminating mind of John shows in the tensed furrowing of his brow and the locking of his chiseled, stubble-dusted jaw as he clenches and unclenches his teeth, chewing on nothing but his worries.

"Then we'll let the hover propulsion stabilize our fall," he says, finishing my sentence, "provided there aren't too many trees."

"Yes, that's it," I encourage him over the wailing alarm, my small, pale hand still resting on his rough one.

As the belly of the craft flirts with the fog, the hum of its engine grows louder. Then everything starts to shiver, from the walls to the tied-down crates to our very feet, as if cutting through the cloud is its most trying endeavor yet. The white blanket rises, rises, rises … until white is all we know.

Instantly, the dark trees emerge through the blinding white, appearing as ugly, crooked thorns jutting out of the earth and whipping past us. Too soon, the craft grazes the tips of the trees, snapping them right off and showering splinters down below. Shaking, jostling, we all clutch our nearest savior—a crate, a chair, a person—and brace for a less-than-tender landing.

The ground rushes to meet the vehicle faster than any of us can scream, but before we crash, the propulsion of the hovercraft makes us bounce off the ground, then ricocheting sideways off a thicket of nearby trees, and then the whole craft goes belly-up, all of us flipped upside-down. Losing my footing, I clutch John as we tumble to the ceiling—our new floor—and are met with the slam of Marianne's body to my right. The three of us squeezed against the screens of the ceiling that blink and flicker and flash, we hold on tightly as everything slows to an abrupt and noiseless stop.

The lights flicker off, the alarm ceasing with it.

In the merciful silence, we hear the engine breathe its last, almost like a sigh, and then we are truly in a silent nothingness. Even our breathing seems trapped in a vacuum, my heartbeat turned silent as we lie in the dark.

Mari is first to speak. "Jen? John?"

"I'm alive," I answer quietly.

"I'm good," John returns too. I feel his body shift, perhaps to lift his head. "Delivery guy? You still with us?"

He responds with a miserable and meek, "Mm-hmm," before he, too, squirms in the dark to right himself.

I lift my own head, looking in all directions, hungry for a sign of light. Even the front window lends nothing; everything in all directions is pure black. When my eyes adjust, I catch a dim red glimmer in my peripheral and turn toward it to find Mari's glowing cheeks staring back at me. With a grunt, I pull out my device that still lives in my pocket. The miniscule light that emits from its screen casts a ghostly glow that fills the cabin.

"Can we get a better light?" asks John. "I don't want you to waste its energy. We may need it."

"This is all your fault," whimpers the boy, his voice quivering. "We're all dead and it's your fault."

I'm not quite sure to whom he's assigning said fault, but I'll assume it's me. I'm about to say something when John answers instead. "We're not dead," he tells him, like it's good news. "We're all safe, all alive. I know you didn't plan to do this when you woke up this morning, but we're all in this together now whether we want to be or not." When thc boy doesn't answer, John sighs and says, "I know you're scared. We all are, but if you stick with us, you'll be safe."

"Safe," repeats the boy quietly. The cabin is silent for a moment. Then, he says, "You needed a light. I have this." He crawls over the ceiling to hand John a wristlet, of which he holds two. John takes one and slaps it on his wrist, wrinkling his brow and jabbing a finger at it, confused. "You press right here on the top," he tells John, demonstrating, "and then it—"

A beam of light pours out, stabbing the opposite wall.

"Bright," John grunts—or maybe complains, I can't tell—then climbs to his feet to survey the cabin. "Why'd the hovercraft just shut off like that?" he asks himself.

The boy answers the rhetorical question. "It's just a

defensive feature of any hovercraft. They aren't meant to be upside-down ever, so it shuts off to p-p-prevent further damage and ensure the safety of its passengers. Thrusters are only on its underside." He scrounges in the dark for his lost cap, reclaiming it near the back of the cabin.

"So you *do* know a thing or two," remarks John. "Wait. Are you telling me we have to flip this whole thing over for it to work again?"

"I don't *know*," the boy grumbles tiredly. "The four of us alone can't dream of budging a *hovercraft*. Look at me! I struggle to even carry a simple shipping crate! That's why they left me behind to watch the ship!" On his feet now, he gives the wall a frustrated kick. "Great and wonderful job I did of that. I'm *so* fired."

"You can't lift a crate, and they hired you as a delivery boy?"

The boy's pouty, resentful eyes are his only answer.

Impatient, I push forward to the controls, which now rest on the ceiling. Looking up at them, I spot the button that once closed the ramp and reach for it.

"Jen!" hisses Mari. "What are you doing??"

I smirk. "Opening the door. What's it look like?"

"Stop! No!"

I sigh and stare back at my friend. "What's our plan, then? Huddle in here all day and braid each other's hair? Why don't we see where we've landed, at the very least?

Explore our surroundings. Then, we'll come back inside and close up for the night, using this craft as our … base. Hell, it's stocked with enough food for weeks, isn't it?"

"A month, maybe more," the boy agrees, counting the crates with his eyes. "Split among four of us, hmm …"

"We may need to seek out a source of water, too," I point out, itching to have a look around. "I can't believe we're here," I murmur with exhilaration, half to myself. "The realm of the Dead. The place I've only heard about since I was a child. The place of—"

"A source of *water* …?!" cries Marianne, exasperated. "Did you leave your brain back on campus?? A complete and utter *lack* of resources is the very reason this place is what it is! No food anywhere. Every river has run dry. The shore is toxic. The trees are dead. I'm worried even the *air* out there is poison."

I don't share her worries, and she clearly doesn't share my excitement. "Well, there's only one way to find out." I reach for the button.

"JEN!"

A faint groan comes from the engine, then the door above us opens up, spilling in a hazy light from outside.

"See? We're not dead yet," I tell Mari. "The craft is just sleeping, not powerless. She'll open and close when we want. Let's have a look around, then we'll be back to eat some dinner. I could go for a little bit of what we had before we left. How about you?" I put on a chipper smile, then climb atop a crate to reach the exit, ignoring Mari's utterly stupefied expression.

When I raise my head through the threshold, my eyes are met with splinters of darkness and grey. The thick blanket of mist, which looked so bright from above, casts quite a shadow underneath that is bleak and heavy. I take the splinters to be trees, and not inviting ones at that. My excitement, quite quickly, becomes apprehension. This is what it looks like … during the day?

John appears right next to me and aims his wrist, a spear of light cutting through the dark. It does nothing to make our surroundings any more welcoming. It just worsens the gloom, bringing to light the eerie trees, knobbed, gnarled, and misshapen as they are. Mari joins us at last, her eyes opened brightly. To my surprise, she seems more fascinated than terrified, staring out into the nothing. That, or her eyes still have yet to adjust.

None of us say a word. We're waiting for something to happen. John turns his light left, turns his light right, aiming and searching … for what?

Then I see it. Two tiny white specks.

Before I can draw enough breath for a decent scream, the shadows in the dark leap upon us. I throw my hands forward, catching—*something*—by the throat, and then I hold on for dear life. I don't hold on for long. The *thing's* momentum topples me, sending me right back into the craft. Landing on my back with a sickening grunt, I twist my face away while the—*claws, talons, severely-unkempt fingernails*—try their very best to tear out my eyes.

Mari's scream reaches my ears suddenly, and that seems to inspire a little fight into my muscles. With a thrust, I overturn the dark figure and straddle it. Atop the creature, I pin it to the floor of the craft—or rather, the ceiling—and emit a belly-given war cry into its faceless face while I attempt to strangle it to death.

That doesn't last long. The creature lurches somehow and I'm on my back again, the creature hissing with a mad intent, its arms quivering as it holds me down.

A sudden beam of light dresses our faces for a brief moment, and in this brief moment, I find I'm strangling the thin neck of a young man with pale blue eyes and pasty chapped lips. His eyebrows—one of which seems half-shaven—are pulled up in surprise, and I have a sudden thought that I might be wrestling with a fellow human who's been stranded here in the lightless realm.

He seems to think similarly of me, because his grip softens when our eyes meet. He draws no breath and says no word, but his pale eyes continue to bore into mine, curious and searching.

What is he searching for?

A blunt object to the pale boy's head terminates said

search, throwing him across the cabin. Standing over me now is John, who lends a hand to help me up.

Before I can even take it, the creature-boy is back on his feet, tackling John to the wall. I shriek and clamber to my feet, stumbling out of the way as John and the *thing* wrestle back and forth. John gains footing, shoving the boy into a crate, but then the boy propels himself off the crate and slams John into the opposite wall with an inhuman growl that sounds almost catlike. John grapples for something with his free hand, catches grip of a sharp lever connected to—*something*—then rips it out of the wall and twists the creature-boy around in one deft move, stabbing the boy's hand into the wall.

Shockingly, the boy seems to feel no pain—that, or he's too riled up on adrenaline to feel anything at all—but with one of his hands stuck to the wall, he has only the other with which to claw at John. Taking no chances, John moves to take another lever off of the control panel, but finds it not as willing to let go as the first one was, so he goes for the nearest food crate, quickly unbinding it. Then, with a grunt and an impressive strain of muscle, John shoves the crate at the pale boy, crushing his legs against the wall and effectively trapping him.

With most of his body pinned to the wall and only one hand free, the pasty *boy-thing* seems to process his predicament quickly, giving up the pursuit of scratching out our eyeballs, and just stares at us as he hangs there.

John breathes heavy, leaning against the wall, calming down. I note a scratch on my left arm, but ignore its sting, much preferring to keep my attention on our capture.

A soft moan comes from the ramp where Marianne wrings her hands and peers around outside, her big eyes shivering with unease. "I … I don't see …"

"The other one got away," John finishes for her.

"Other one?" I blurt. "There was another one?"

"I fought it," John confirms. "The thing got scared, it looked like. Ran off."

"It was a f-f-female," says Mari.

John snorts. "No, it wasn't. It was bald, which was about the only thing I could see before it leapt at me."

"She had breasts and a woman's *hips*," she argues.

"That thing wasn't man *or* woman."

I take one hesitant step forward. "Does he talk?" I ask, then face the pale creature to find out for myself. "Hi," I say gently. "You just tried to kill me. My name is Jennifer. He's John, the one who just stabbed you into the wall. That's my friend Marianne by the door in the ceiling, but you can call her Mari. And … sorry, delivery boy, but you never told us your name. Want to introduce yourself?"

John and Mari look at me as if I've just turned into a tarantula.

"East," answers the delivery boy. "Connor Easton, but

they c-c-call me East, they all call me East."

I return my gaze to the creature on the wall. "Do you have a name?" I ask.

He just hangs there without a word, the wet whites of his eyes flicking between us suspiciously. He's probably wondering what we're going to do with him.

"What are we going to do with him?" asks our trusty delivery boy East, who quivers in the corner of the room clutching his own light-spraying wristlet, as if protectively shielding the light from us.

"Figure out what the hell it is," says John, staring at it with a mixture of disgust and anger.

"We know what it is," I retort, annoyed at his obvious denial. "We know what *he* is." I face the pale boy again. "Can you talk?"

The creature does not.

"Are you …" I take a short breath. Though the boy-thing does not immediately reek of anything foul as one would naturally expect, his appearance still encourages a great sense of reluctance to breathe near him. "Are you … Undead?"

The creature still says nothing. He almost pouts, as if disappointed that he's been captured.

John huffs, annoyed. "The other one could come back any second. We have to capture it too before it kills us."

"These were once people," I assert. "He's scared. I'm

sure the other one is scared, too. We've invaded their … *habitat* … without their consent. They have a right to exercise certain precautions."

"Certain precautions? Like ripping our throats out?"

I shoot John a look. "We need to respect them. They are people."

"They *were* people. I don't know what *that* is," he says with a careless flick of his hand. "It was going at me like it wanted to sink its teeth into my neck. This was a mistake, all of this."

"What?"

"We shouldn't have come." John huffs, mad suddenly. "We're going to die out here in the middle of nowhere. That other one's going to wait until we're asleep and it's going to hunt us and pull our bowels out of our bellies."

"John …"

He's out of the cabin the next instant, pushing past Mari, I guess to look for the one that got away. I stare after him for a moment, hurt by his brashness. *Is he right?* I have to wonder. *Have I brought us all out here to die?*

Mari's face reflects a similar trepidation. When my gaze meets hers, I feel my resolve break further. "I know, I know, you're mad at me too, but—"

"I'm just in sh… shock," whispers Mari, her voice weary and halfway gone from screaming. "I expected … I expected us to get here and … and embark on a long search through wild, magical wilderness for days before finding proof of the Living Dead. I hadn't expected to find it so," her purple eyes meet the creature's, "quickly."

I turn back. The boy's pale, ghostly eyes haven't left mine, and though his dry, abraded lips still curl with half a snarl contained behind them, I sense a calmness in his face that wasn't there before. Is he coming to trust me?

"There's nothing to be afraid of," I tell this creature, who we've half-crushed against the wall by a heavy metal crate and stabbed one of his hands in place by a sharp lever that belongs in a computer somewhere. "The four of us are only visiting and will be gone soon. We don't—"

"Five."

The sudden word cuts like an icicle to the chest. His voice is unexpectedly deep and crystal clear. "Five?" I shake my head. "There's only four of us. Myself, Mari—"

"Five," the creature repeats, then inhales deeply and inclines his head toward the back of the cabin like a dog smelling meat.

Mari, Easton, and I turn our eyes. The darkness in the back of the craft returns our stare with silence.

Then, the shadows speak: "Don't hurt me."

East emits a shriek of surprise, backing away.

"Who's there?" I call out into the dark, sounding about ninety percent braver than I feel. "Show yourself!"

The person—a woman, if I had to guess by the sound

of her voice—remains exactly where she is, unseen. "So, so, so, so sorry," she whimpers. "Please. I didn't mean—I don't want to—I was only—"

"Who are you??" I demand.

"It's me!"

"Who's 'me'??"

Then, ever slowly, the darkness parts, and from the shadows of an overturned crate, a thin and bony woman emerges. She is dressed in silks, and her hair is so bushy, it appears like a hundred writhing snakes. Then—

I blink. "D-Dana …?"

Dana the Diviner's eyes grow wide. "I only meant to speak with you back at campus, and … and I thought that, maybe I'd—"

"How'd you get here??" I gape, unable to place when the hell she could've boarded our craft. "Did you follow me? Have … Have you been aboard this whole time??"

"I couldn't just let you *go*," says the woman, her eyes turning dark. "What you did to me was unforgiveable. And what you were *going* to do—"

"They're coming."

I turn to the pale boy, whose ominous words bring my heart to full racing speed without even knowing their meaning. "Who's coming?" I ask at once.

"All of them," he answers.

The next instant, John's reappeared at the opening.

"Shut the door and lock up. *Now,*" he says quickly, out of breath from running. "It's so dark out there, but I saw other ones approaching. Lots and lots of them."

"Hair as white as winter …" breathes the boy, his eyes turning hungry and a wicked smile finding his face.

My eyes dart around, having adjusted to the unsettling semidarkness. "The front window is broken," I point out. "They might pry open the ramp from the outside, I can't be sure. Oh, no. They could just … They could easily …"

"Crawl in," finishes the boy, a hint of victory in his deep voice. "Climb in. Claw in."

"We have to run," John says and realizes at the same time, and even he can't hide the terror that's flooding his eyes. "Pack a bag. Food. As much as you can carry."

The boy closes his eyes, grinning. "They're already *here, here, here …*"

Something slams against the outside of the craft. The groan of a hungry *something* bleeds through the metal, a groan that sends deadly shivers up my back. At once, I clamber for the opening, desperate to shut it, but John grips it tight and says, "This vehicle isn't *safe!* We have to *run,* Jennifer!"

"No!" I yell out, my knees shaking. "We're safe in here! We have food! It's suicide if we leave this vehicle!"

"It's suicide if we *don't!*"

Marianne, making the decision for all of us, plunges

out of the vehicle and vanishes from sight. My heart's ripped out of my chest the moment she goes, and the first horrible thought that passes through my head is: *I'll never see her again*. I can't let that happen, so I seize John's wrist and charge headfirst out of the hovercraft and into the patient, hungry dark.

Chapter Three

A Roof Would Be Nice

I swallow an impulsive shout for Marianne to slow down or let me know how far she's gone, knowing that my every sound is a weakness when countless Undead are hunting the scent of my delicious Living blood. Soon, I'm running side by side with John through the tall black trees that, in the dark, all seem to be laughing at me. I pray my feet will keep me quick and that nothing underfoot will trip me. Any stumble could mean my death.

There are footsteps behind us. After seeing how fast the pale boy had moved, I know these are not the slowly staggering zombies of fiction and folklore; these people are just like me except they're … well, dead. They run. They fear. And worst of all, they hunger. I don't like to venture what they enjoy for a typical supper.

"Light," breathes John, seeing it at the same time I do.

"Maybe they're afraid of it," I say, praying I'm right, but not willing to bet anyone's toes on it.

We break through the scourge of trees, dumping onto

the most dismal beach I've ever seen. The sand is the color of dust, like an ashen shore that doesn't welcome the ocean, but instead seems to push it away as though it were some gross experiment offered to you at dinner by your sweet, well-meaning Aunt Belinda. The water is less appealing than the beach, falling somewhere on the color wheel between blue-grey and the precise color of *murk*.

"Where's Mari??" I ask at once, scanning the shore and finding no sign of my friend.

John grips my hand and keeps me moving toward the water. Just before our feet touch the ocean, we pull back, both of us likely sharing the same thought: *I don't want to know what happens to my skin when it touches those foul, contaminated waters.*

We turn at the sound of feet kicking sand and find East and the Diviner Dana breaking from the grim line of trees. A moment later, they've joined us by the water, and the four of us stare back at the row of needle-sharp, lifeless foliage that wait, silent as death.

"Where's Mari?" I ask again, my stomach twisting. "East? Did you see my friend?" His blue eyes quiver when he shakes his head no, confirming my fears. "Oh, no …"

"She could still be running," reasons John. "She might be hiding in a thicket of trees. She might be—"

"Dead."

The word comes from Dana. At the sound of it, I snap

and round about upon her, furious. "How the hell did you get on that ship??" I demand.

She lifts a hand. "The spirit world spoke to me. I knew precisely where you'd be, and why. I've come to—"

"You *followed* us, liar," I blurt right back, cutting her off. "I don't know how, but I know you snuck onto that ship right behind us. How'd I not hear you??"

Dana frowns. "You were arguing at the control panel. There was an empty food crate in the back. I hid."

"Food!" I cry out, my mind thrust into a different and far more pressing direction. "Oh, no! All of our *food* is on that craft! How are we going to survive??"

The delivery boy makes a sound and taps a satchel that I only now discover hangs from his shoulders. "I took as much as I could." He stares at the ground miserably. "It isn't much."

I drop to my knees in the sand, staring at the forest in mute horror. *I've brought us here to die*, I tell myself, my favorite thing to tell myself lately. Already, Marianne …

"We can't stop moving," says John, "because *they* sure as hell won't."

"The spirit world is awakened," agrees Dana airily.

"Let's go, Jennifer. We have to go."

We resume our hurrying right where we left off, pushing feet into the stubborn sand and moving laterally, skirting the edges of the dark woods. The sand makes running difficult, breaking and crumbling beneath our feet. I keep stealing glances at the woods, terrified that the creatures are going to find us. Their eyes could be hidden between the trees, watching as we make our futile escape.

And every step I take is another step I'm putting between my friend Marianne and I. How can I just leave her out there, running through the woods all alone? What kind of person does that? Likely someone who would hear of her father's dying and, instead of running to comfort her mother, throws herself right into peril.

I'm a glutton for horror. And a selfish one, at that.

"Keep going," John calls from behind, encouraging us. "No slacking, Connor. We have to keep moving."

"They … call … me … East," the boy replies between breaths.

"They'll call you dead if you slow down."

Suddenly, I've had it with the guilt in my chest. "No!" I cut away from the others, plunging towards the forest.

John cries out for me, but I ignore him. I won't leave Marianne behind. I won't run for my life, not when someone else's could be lost. Maybe I'm purely motivated by guilt and this isn't some brave, heroic thing I'm doing. Maybe I'd much rather be lying around in my condo complaining about my professors and the food they serve at the cafeteria and my fast-crumbling thesis. Maybe I'd rather be looking at my mom in the holograph, mourning the loss of my dad and reminiscing on the good old days.

But this is my life's work. This is the reason I'm alive. And I brought these people here with me to gather proof of the Dead. I won't let us join them as fellow corpses-with-appetites.

John calls for me again, and from the sound of his voice, I know he's following me. *Better stop shouting unless it's your intention to draw all the Living Dead towards us*, I think just as the world grows dark again and the great deathly blanket of mist above becomes my new and permanent sky.

The trees are endless in all directions, if I can even dignify these dead black things with the word "tree". I fumble in the semidarkness, my hands thrown up to grab a trunk and prevent my fall. Frozen against the tree, I listen.

John stops running too, coming up to my back and standing still so his feet no longer make a noise. I don't turn around to see him, knowing he's smart enough to catch on to my intent.

Nothing, I think miserably to myself. *I hear nothing*. I scan the twisted environs, searching for a sign of anything alive *or* dead. I listen with all my might, desperate to catch wind of even the slightest whisper of breath or crackle of branch underfoot.

Snap! I hear it, and charge.

John is right on my heels—and this time, he has sense enough not to shout my name. I don't even know what I'm racing towards. Is it friend or foe? When I find it, will it greet me with a sigh of relief or try to eat my face?

"Jennifer," he breathes in my ear.

I see the same thing he sees before another word's exchanged. In the distant dark, the unmistakable gleam of eyes find mine. Many eyes. Four sets of them. Five ... I can't count. The moment they see me, they move. *Well, I'm no good to Marianne if I'm dead*, I reason, and with all the bravery I just gathered up, I find myself running away from them again.

"This way!"

East is leading the way suddenly—I hadn't realized he and Dana were still with us—and our meek and very-alive party of four cuts through the dark in the direction East is taking us. Hopefully it's a direction with a happy ending.

The trees end abruptly, revealing a long and winding riverbank. The water is shockingly dark with sheets of glossy film that float upon its surface.

East seems not to be daunted by the utterly repulsive sight, thrusting himself through its vile waters to get to the other side. After a quick look at one another, John and I swallow our vanity and go in right after him. The feel of the water against my legs is less like water and more like a thick and strangely icy oil. The further the water comes up, the higher I raise my hands, desperate not to touch any more of it to my skin than I have to. To my waist it comes, then to my chest as I move further and further across the river. Then my feet give away on the soft riverbed, pulling me into the disgusting water up to my chin. I give out a yelp, hearing echoes of my voice slap back at me from all directions, then desperately push myself further and further through the murk.

"John!" I call out.

"Right behind you," he says. "Keep moving."

Just then, I lose my balance again—or else the river itself is alive, cruelly taking my feet from under me—and this time I don't regain any purchase. Submerged totally in the water, I don't dare open my eyes, flailing my slow-motion arms and kicking my stubborn legs. I can't even tell which direction I'm going and, unprepared for the fall, I'm quickly losing what remained of my breath.

A strong pair of arms wrap tight around me, and then I feel myself being dragged along. My head breaks the surface just long enough for a single gasp of air before I'm submerged yet again. After another moment of desperate panicking, my head breaks the surface again. I scream, only to have my head pulled under once more, my mouth filled with river water, if I can ever dare call it that.

I'm going to drown in the land of the Dead.

The next instant, I drop onto the bank, coughing and

spitting out vile water. The arms let go of me and I turn to find John staring down at me, his eyes pouring with hurt and passion, his mouth gaping with his every heavy breath. I stare up into his eyes for a moment, and my first thought is, *I'm so glad you're here with me. You save my little meaningless life over and over again.*

Then I sit up with a start, reminded of our pursuers. To my bafflement, I find a line of five men and women on the opposite riverbank from which we'd come. They each look worse than the other. Among them is the pale boy we'd pinned to the wall of that craft; how he was freed and can still somehow walk, I can only speculate. The five of them stare at us, motionless and stark.

"Why are they just standing there?" John whispers to us, confused.

"The water," answers East. "I suspected it. When I'd quickly filled my satchel from the overturned crate, a canister of water slipped from my hand and spilled in front of one of them. Its reaction was ... well, it was telling. They don't like water. That canister saved my life. I got out of the craft and tore off running, fast as I could."

Water? That's all it takes? I rise, drawing as close to the riverbank as I can, astonished by the fact. Only a hundred feet separates us from the Dead, maybe less. For a while, I can almost convince myself that the five of them are just dirtied, homeless street beggars. Really, except for a few unsightly characteristics, they look … human.

"We have to find shelter somewhere, somehow," says John quietly in my ear.

I step into the water, just to where it comes up to my knees. The curiosity throbs in my chest with my every hungry heartbeat. I want to see them even closer. I want to know them. I want to *understand* them. Do they want to understand me? Surely they haven't seen a Living person in quite some time. Nothing has lived over here—whether plant or animal or otherwise—in hundreds and hundreds of years, if the Histories are to be believed. I can't explain why there's a river here when I thought they'd all dried up, or why we're able to breathe the air, or why there's a thick blanket of fog concealing this land from the sun and, yet, somehow it feels as cold as winter. Just that thought makes me shiver, the murky water still dripping from my hair and chin and fingertips.

"Jennifer," he starts to say again.

I lift my face to the row of Dead, certain they are, in fact, what we suspect they are. "We mean you no harm," I assure them, my voice quivering and small. "We didn't mean to disrupt your way of life—"

"You *are* our way of life."

The response came from the bald one with one eye who stands protectively near the one we'd pinned to the wall of the ship earlier. Mari was right; the bald one has a woman's shape. Even despite the lack of hair and the greyness of her skin, she looks almost pretty.

"What?" I return, unsettled by her response.

The woman says nothing more, simply staring at us from across the dark river. The Dead stand so still, one could easily mistake them for another row of lifeless trees, splinters of grey against the black.

I don't know why I stupidly expected our visit to be so different, as if the Dead were going to welcome us with hot chocolate and marshmallows. I pictured us wandering through a landscape of wonder, visiting quaint villages of happily-living Dead, sitting around campfires and asking about their world. I imagined an exciting adventure that fulfilled the deepest hunger of our curious human spirits; I hadn't expected *us* to fulfill something *else's* hunger.

"We have your big metal bird," adds the woman with a certain snarkiness. "If there was a way across the river, we'd have your blood, too."

"Come," whispers John. "She's just trying to scare us."

"You should be scared," says the woman, hearing him perfectly. She lifts her chin, her one ghostly white eye shining in the dim light cutting through the fog. "They're always scared before they die."

Reluctantly, I let John pull me away from the vile riverbank. My gaze never leaves the bald woman on the other side until the thicket of dead trees eventually blocks her from view. Facing front, I drown in the darkness that lies ahead of me and the grief that lies behind. Soon, the only sound I hear is the careless crunching of our own clumsy Living footsteps. I don't even care if anyone hears us … or any*thing*. I've lost all my thrill of this horrible place, and quite suddenly all I want to do is go home.

And that isn't possible anymore because our big metal bird is on *that* side of the river. Big metal bird. I might prefer that term over hovercraft, except we might have killed said bird. It flew too far from its nest.

And so have we.

After too much time in silence passes, Dana—I still will not speculate how the hell she snuck onto the ship undetected—gives a dramatic spread of her wrinkly hands and then says, "Here, yes?"

It's a small clearing of trees where she's stopped. "Here, what?" I ask, annoyed.

She studies my face, her eyes squeezed with emotion. "The spirits are very calm here," she answers. "They've gone swimming in the mists above, perhaps. We do need a place to recover ourselves for a spell, yes?"

I realize that, despite all of her fake diviner crap, this is actually her attempt at being kind. But why?

"You said something to me earlier," I remind her. "In the ship. You followed me on campus? You—"

"No need to worry about that, now. We're among the

spirits," she says with a wave of her hands. "They sleep, and so should we. We oughtn't be caught by them when they choose to wake. Besides, your friend said it best," she murmurs, her wild eyes flicking to John. "If we stick together, we will be safe, yes?"

How much did she overhear? All of it? "I have no idea what time it even is," I mutter miserably. "Dead of night. Dead of morning." My heart lurches suddenly, my eyes filling with tears that don't drop. "I can't let Mari just—"

"No," says Dana right away. "Your friend is fine, just fine. She is not one with the spirits, otherwise I'd sense her." Dana blinks her big eyes, waves a hand in the air as if to clear it of cobwebs, then adds, "Yes, I see the truth of it. Marigold is most fine. We will reunite with your friend soon, if the spirits are truthful ..."

"Her name is Mari*anne*," I correct her.

"Oh, of course." Dana bites her lip, her face wrinkling. "I wonder why I said the other name."

"We'll need to ration our food," the delivery boy cuts in quietly, hugging his satchel. "I didn't get much." He stares sadly at the ground, his once white uniform now decorated with ashen stains and smears. His third red eyebrow has turned dark, the blood having dried.

"Let's rest, then," I say, despite the incessant pulling in my stomach. I'll have to take Dana's sugar-coated lie as my only comfort. *Please, Marianne ... Please be safe. And if by some miracle you are, then* stay *safe.*

After a little bite of dried, tasteless fruit, and a human function or four done in private behind a tree, we settle in our space for the setting sun—assuming it's setting, as we have no means by which to tell, the greedy fog floating in the way. Dana leans against a knobby charcoaled tree, petting it as though it were telling her a bedtime story that only she hears. East has made a pillow of his satchel, curled into a ball on the ground with his hands tucked between his thighs, and though he's supposed to be sleeping, he's staring despondently at nothing.

John and I share the trunk of a tree at the opposite end of the clearing apart from the other two. His thick arm pushes into my shoulder, but I hardly feel it, picking at my nails and wondering why the hell I didn't plunge right back across that cursed river in search of my friend.

"I'm glad you're with me," I whisper.

John shrugs, the muscles in his shoulder contracting. "I couldn't have let you go alone."

"You could have," I reason. "The food in my condo could have kept you fed for weeks. You could have easily snuck out and gone back home too, if you wanted."

He turns his head. "Huh? No. I'm not going home to face my sad, disappointed parents, not until I'm an official student at the university. We've already gone over this."

"But now, you're a criminal because of me. We're all

criminals. If we ever get back home ..."

"We'll be coming back with proof of the Dead," he reminds me. He brings a hand to my arm, and his fingers brush down the length of it. Pleasant tingles drift through my body. His hand rests on mine, then he turns his body and puts an arm around me, pulling me in close to him. It's the first time in a while that it feels like we're truly alone. I wonder if it's totally inappropriate or selfish of me to want him to kiss me, right here and now.

"You're warm," I realize, tightening my body into his. I hadn't realized how cold I'd gotten. Sometimes it feels like we just met a few days ago. Sometimes it's like I've known him my whole life. "It's so miserable here. I hate the cold. I want to go home."

"We will," he says calmly. "We have to. I'm certain there's some mechanism on that craft that's alerted the university of exactly where it crashed. They'll have a rescue party out to collect us."

I lift my head so my icy eyes fall right into his muddy brown ones. He's so damn handsome, even dirtied up and rugged in the Undead wilderness. "Are you sure?"

"We better have our proof by the time they find us." He smiles. Or, rather, he makes a subtle smirk with his lips, which I know to be *his* version of smiling. John, the eternally brooding, the stoic ...

I bring my lips to his. My heart rushes into my throat.

His hand slips behind my neck, caressing me as I melt apart in his arms. For the first time in a long time, I'm reminded what it felt like when we first met. It was right after my embarrassing speech to my class about the so-named Beautiful Dead, and he gave me a moment's half-distracted consolation before running away from me, escaping the watchful eyes of campus authorities who'd been searching him out for sneaking into classes. That same night, I had a spare ticket to the gardens, and so together we went and created a night for ourselves that neither of us would soon forget.

John shifts his weight, bringing me gently to the ground and crawling over me like an animal. A deep and rumbling growl from within his chest even suggests it more so. *I'm in love with a beast,* I think to myself. And maybe someday he'll say the same back to me … sans "beast", that is. He looks down on me with hunger in his eyes. *Right here?* I want to ask, astonished. *In the middle of the realm of the Dead? In view of the two others?* He seems to read my thoughts, a wicked smirk twisting his face as he watches the emotions race across mine. Then he kisses me, and I'm lost in the taste of this beautiful man.

His energy soon expires, and we collapse to the ashen ground holding each other in the semidarkness, which grows darker and darker by the minute.

"That was a lie just to comfort me, wasn't it?" I ask

quietly. "The part about a rescue crew from the university coming to save us?"

He only clutches me tighter and rests his chin upon my head. The sight of his gently rising and falling chest is the last thing I see before drifting off.

When my eyes open, I've no doubt that the night has fallen. *I shouldn't be sleeping*, I tell myself, blinking my eyes. *I'll sleep enough when I'm dead.* A chill runs through my body from the tips of my toes to the end of my nose. I realize John's grip on me has loosened and he now holds more of himself than anything else, hugging his chest tightly as he dreams. The two others still rest on the other side of the clearing, the boy with his satchel-pillow and Dana leaning against her new best friend: a big dead tree.

Soundlessly, I rise to my feet and turn around in a full circle. Every direction shows me the same impenetrable darkness. Gosh, it's so damn inviting, I wonder why we're not all sightseeing right now.

Then, I spot a light. My face twists, doubting it at first. What could possibly be glowing in the woods? One of the diviner's spirits? Despite my inner amusement, I can't bring myself to smile. The subtle light worries me.

My eyes grow double. *It's Marianne*, I realize at once. The light almost glows red as her cheeks, except …

Recklessly, I move through the woods in pursuit. The forest floor snaps beneath my feet every five or six paces, but the light makes no sound at all. *Am I mistaken?*

It grows dimmer and greyer, losing its color. It's as if the light retreats the closer I get. Maybe it's just an illusion reflected off the thick and sleepless clouds above my head, perhaps casting an image of the moon into the woods below. Is it a full moon, or am I being lured to my death?

"Mari?" I call out, my voice quivering with anxiety. "Is that you? Mari?"

I stop. The shifting grey light takes the shape of a person, not my friend's glowing red cheek, and quite suddenly it looks like someone else entirely. My eyes fill with tears and I bring a hand to my mouth. Is he who I think he is? Is he …

"Dad?" I whisper through my shaking fingers.

The light moves, dancing across the trees the way a reflection bends and twists through unrested waters. I watch it with shock, overcome by what I'm seeing. Have I gone as mad as Dana, or is there merit to her powers? The shape draws closer, closer …

Then it's not my father at all. I step away at once, my back slamming into a tree as the pale, dead-eyed boy is upon me.

Chapter Four

Heart Beater

Just as I fill my lungs for a scream, the creature presses his gross dead finger to my lips, then freezes. He doesn't hiss or growl. He doesn't bare his teeth. He doesn't move but for the grey finger he just put to my mouth.

It's the same pale boy we captured in the hovercraft. I try not to be repulsed by his cold dead digit on my lips.

"No hard feelings?" I quietly ask through the finger.

"Just me," he whispers. "No sister."

"The other one ... is your sister?" I ask, putting it together. "The one with no hair and one eye? The one who threatened to eat us from across the river?"

His eyes scan down my neck, then my body, then return to my face appearing thrice as hungry as before. I guess the word "eat" inspired a thought in his Dead brain. I ought to be more choosy with my words.

Realizing, however, that he has refrained from eating me thus far, I find myself curious. "What do you want?"

He puckers his lips, considering my question. For a

moment, he doesn't seem to know the answer. I see the conflict in his face. Maybe I'm still not so safe from being eaten after all.

"Is it my friend?" I ask with fleeting hope. "Marianne? Have you come to tell me you have her and you want to propose some sort of bargain for us to get her back? Is that it? Have you come to strike some sort of Undeadly deal?"

The pale boy studies me long and hard. Maybe it's the emotion John stirred within me before we fell asleep the night before, but I find myself surprised by my reaction to this … person. He has oddly pretty, soft eyes, even with their pale coloring. Though I know what he might intend to do, I find myself trusting that, in truth, he doesn't want to harm me. I hope it isn't foolish to believe that.

"No deal," he whispers.

"Please," I beg him, unable to be strong right now. "Please, if you have her, if you have my friend, *please* return her to me. She wasn't even supposed to come with me. She doesn't deserve to die."

"You *all* deserve to die."

"No, no, no." I feel my insides lurching. I can already picture my friend brutally murdered in a million different ways. Eviscerated. Sliced in half. Bitten upon every inch of her body. The sound of her last screams. "Please," I beg him again. "Return Marianne to me. I beg you! That's why you've come, isn't it? Have you brought her with you? Oh, please, *please* tell me you—"

"I've come alone."

I stare at him with hurt in my eyes, breathing heavily. "Will you ... tell me at least if she's ... alive?"

He stares at me for too long. In this moment, his pale eyes nearly turn human, touched by a strand of feelings that seem to run through him. Then, in a whisper that I almost doubt I hear, he says: "Yes."

Oh, thank you. *Thank you, thank you, thank you.* But that means they have her, or else she got away and is on the run. That means ... "How'd you get over the water?"

"There is a place down the river where the trees reach for one another," he says, his full, chapped lips never quite closing as he speaks, "and I am braver than the others. I am agile. I am light."

"The others didn't follow?"

"The others don't know the path," he says, "and if they do, they don't risk it. One slip, and you drop."

"What happens when you touch the water?" The little researcher in me has come out of her office. "I didn't read anything about water in my studies."

"Your ... studies?" The boy's eyes narrow, suspicious of the word.

"I'm from the land of the ... um, the *alive*," I explain, unsure what to call it. "It's across the ocean. That way." I point, though in truth, I'm so turned around that I have no idea which way I'm pointing. "I'm just a student at the school there."

"School?"

"Part of my studies," I go on, "include people like … well, people like *you*. And I—"

"Like me," he echoes, his face turning dark.

I worry I'm not making my situation any better. "See, the people over there, the alive-people, they don't think people like *you* exist. They don't believe in the Beautiful Dead. That's what I call you," I add, feeling suddenly self-conscious about the term. "Sorry. I just—"

"*Beautiful*," he hisses, shutting me right up. His lips contort into a snarl. Then, too close to my face, he says, "There is nothing *beautiful* about me."

I look into his strange, otherworldly eyes. "I disagree," I reply in half a hush, my breath stolen from me.

The very next instant, the pale boy takes yet another blunt object to the head, and to the ground he goes. In his place stands John breathing heavily and palming a big metal canister. The pale boy, despite being knocked to the ground, doesn't seem fazed in the least; he's already twisting his body around to get back on his feet.

John, however, did not come alone. East holds a metal canister of his own, and he's pulled off the top and holds it threateningly. I don't catch the significance of this oddly dramatic gesture until I see the boy recoil against a tree, staring at the canister with wide, resentful eyes.

"Make one move," John dares him, "and my buddy here will douse you in water and I suspect that will *hurt*."

The boy scowls defiantly, but the fear in his eyes betrays him. I put a hand on John's arm. "John …"

"What were you thinking??" he cries out, turning on me suddenly. I jerk back, surprised. "Why did you come out here all by yourself?"

"I saw—John, I saw a light. I thought it was—"

"We cannot separate!" he shouts, furious with me. "We're vulnerable out here! We are *not* home, Jennifer! Has that fact escaped you?"

"No, John," I bite back, annoyed by the scolding. "I know very well where we are, thank you, but I thought maybe Marianne had—"

"And you didn't think to wake me?! You could've died, Jennifer!" He fumes, his eyes wet with despair. "Are you really so desperate to join your father??"

I slap him. The ringing sound of hand meeting cheek echoes through the woods, taking with it every last word he had left to utter. His jowls shake and he looks away, his face going red. The silence that follows is worse than the silence before when I'd only thought a spirit of my dead dad was coming to find me.

"Maybe so," I whisper, cold as ice.

"Jen …"

I move to the pale boy on the ground, crouching to bring my face closer to his—but not too close. "What do I call you?" I ask him calmly, determined not to let my dumb Living emotions break my resolve.

He only glares at the fell metal canister, which East still loyally holds above his head, ready to dump it.

"I wish to give you the dignity of a name," I explain. "Unless you want me to call you Corpsey, or Dead Guy, or Bad Breath, you need to tell me your name."

For the first time, he pulls his attention from the canister. Then, with a wrinkle of his face, he says, "Bad Breath? I don't breathe."

"I can't imagine it'd be pleasant if you did."

He looks up to consider the canister, and perhaps his whole situation too. "My sister and I haven't called each other by our names in so long. They were given to us … literally … a lifetime ago." Quite suddenly, he looks sad. "I've told myself my own story so many hundreds of times, I'm not even sure it's real anymore. Was I ever alive? Was I ever …" He trails off, lost in his own horror.

I sigh. "Corpsey it is, then."

"They're coming."

The words are Dana's, who I hadn't noticed standing behind East until now. She wrings her hands and her eyes dart around the woods in wonder.

I lift an eyebrow. "Who?"

"Oh, no," groans the pale boy, hugging himself as if a sudden chill had taken him. "You have to let me go. I can't be here. They'll end me. Oh, no. I ... I ..."

"Who is it??" I urge him to tell me.

The canister utterly forgotten, the pale boy clambers to his feet and makes a move to run. John snaps out of a trance that may or may not be him stewing over his prior burst of emotion and my unexpected slap, then tackles the boy to the ground. East shudders, reacting too slow, and some of the water spills upon the Dead boy's feet, though it didn't appear intentional. His feet hiss instantly, smoke swirling up like foggy white snakes, and the scream that bellows from the pale boy's mouth is enough to stir the Dead awake in a three mile radius.

"Tell us!" I demand, calling out over his screams. "Tell us who's coming!"

The shadows part with the soft crunching of footsteps. Dana and East and I back away, terrified by whatever it is that comes our way—something that even *the flesh-eating Dead boy is afraid of.* I mourn the lack of a weapon. I find myself uttering a hundred silent prayers under my breath. I beg for a last sip of my favorite beverage before I die.

Then, a sweet face emerges. A big, bright-eyed, perky-lipped, powdery-white woman's face, framed with yellow hair that curls at the chin. Her lips create a perfect O, and this strange woman says, "Oh my! That noise!"

"I … I'm so sorry," I tell the woman, studying her with curiosity. "We … We didn't mean to disturb you, or your woods, or your …" She looks so beautiful. For a Dead person, that is. "See, we accidentally spilled water on this boy's feet. I apologize for his screaming, but I—"

"Oh, no," says the woman calmly through the boy's agonized cries. "It isn't *his* noise I hear. It's yours!" she says merrily, then turns her face to East and Dana. "And yours! And yours! Ooh …" Her big lips pucker up at the sight of John. "And most definitely *yours*, the noisiest of all! My, my, you're handsome." She giggles suddenly, her eyes shyly drinking in the sight of John, and then she addresses me. "Heart Beaters! You're all Heart Beaters!"

I bring a hand up to my chest protectively, as if I've suddenly become self-conscious of my being alive.

The woman's expression changes, a flash of hurt crossing her face. "Oh, my poor little Heart Beaters. Don't be afraid. We *love* your kind. You make us Undead feel so very special. Please, come with me to the city."

Instantly, my body tingles with excitement and all of my breath is stolen away. Is *this* the Beautiful Dead I've been looking for all along? "C-City? You have a c-c-city?"

"And walls, too! The woods are much too miserable. Hasn't the gloom sucked out all your happiness yet? Oh." She pays mind to John suddenly. "Don't worry, you strong, strapping, handsome young man, you," she says, her eyes turning coy and silly again. "We will take care of the *savage* that tried to harm you."

The word "we" sends a jolt of alarm through me. Two large figures spill from the darkness, but they, like her, look nothing like the Dead we've encountered. One is a brawny man dressed only in jeans, his big bare chest exposed. He has a bald head and a beard with a ring hanging heavily from his nose. The other is a man just as big and bare-chested, but he has a head of long black hair to his shoulders and his eyes are oddly colorless. The two men approach the pale boy and, the moment John dares to back away from them, the men have hold of the boy who still moans in agony from the steam that dances off his ankles. The men drag him into the darkness beyond the woman, whose expression is a sad one. Soon, the sound of the men and the boy is but a whisper of an echo through the dead woods.

"I'm certain we can find a place for you to rest in our city," the woman goes on, unfazed and still appearing full of wonder as she observes us—particularly when she looks at John, who I think she's fast forming an Undeadly crush on.

"How do you expect us to go with you?" asks John, his voice bleeding with mistrust. "Your kind *eat* our kind. We've just narrowly escaped—"

"No, no, no." She shakes her head, wrinkling her lips

in disgust. "No, no, no, no. *They* eat your kind. That boy we just took away. *They* are the little thorns in our fingers, I'm afraid. The people of my city do not practice that sort of … *archaic* practice." She shudders. "Our kind do not need to eat a *thing* to survive. Besides, you'll be in the company of other Heart Beaters! At least ten or twenty."

"Ten or twenty??" I blurt. "There are others alive?"

"Yes, of course! They always find their way to us. I hear most of them come from the land on the other side of the *ocean*." She says the word with such bright, sparkly fascination. "Big metal flying machines deposit them here, though they are most unfortunately deposited, like you, in the middle of the *unkind* parts of our realm. Please," she says with a wave of her hand, "come with me. I insist."

Big metal birds? Others have flown here, too? Like us? *We've been lied to*, I realize. *We've all been lied to. They've known about the Dead's existence this whole time.* Maybe the seven or eight are scientists from our side of the world, coming here to gather samples. They have to be; there's no other explanation.

"Jennifer …"

"Yes," I say at once, ignoring John's quiet protesting. "Yes, of course, I read of you. This is how the Dead are supposed to be. The Beautiful Dead. Never eating, never sleeping. *This* is what we came here for." I face the others. "Cities of happily-living Dead. Sound familiar? Civilized societies of Living Dead. Hygienically-aware Dead."

"*Un*dead," the woman offers politely, "but really, it's sort of the same." She frowns, considering if it is.

"Jen, please."

Despite every misgiving I should share with the others, I keep a tenacity about myself and confidently go with the woman. I came here with but one purpose, and that was to prove the existence of the Beautiful Dead. My first few minutes here proved that very thing, though they weren't so beautiful, and now I have the opportunity of a lifetime. *Death*time. This woman may be my bridge to the wealth of knowledge I've so desperately sought after my whole life; I would be a fool not to chase it.

"The other people, the ones who are alive," I go on, asking. "Are they scientists? Are they just visiting?"

"Oh, I'm afraid I don't know, dear. They don't say much, if I might be blunt as a stone," the woman confesses. "The great metal bird leaves them here and flies away. Always arriving, they are, never seeming to leave. Mmm, it's difficult to find food for your kind in our land," she adds sadly. "It is a bit of a wonder how they survive their stay in our land."

That sounds odd, the part about them being left here. None of it makes sense. "You don't look like the Undead we've encountered," I remark. "Why are you different?"

"We care about our appearance and quality of life,"

she explains cheerfully. "The *savages* who live in the trees and *hunt* like a pack of animals, they deserve what they get, I'm afraid. They are sensitive to certain metals, we've learned, though we can't quite deduce why. That's why our gates and walls are made of metal!"

"That's reassuring," I say, glancing back at East and Dana and John who seem less than enthusiastic to agree.

"You will find yourself quite welcomed, and I say that with no due irony or ulterior meaning," sings the woman, who seems to gain a merry bounce in her step. "We *adore* those with noise in their bodies. The noisier the better," she remarks, giving a sly look and a wink at John. "Oh, how strong and *noisy* you are," she tells him with a giggle, then her face turns sad. "Believe it or not, eternal life can be quite boring."

I risk asking the question that I've let burn inside me since the moment she mentioned seven or eight others. "Have you found any *other* Heart Beaters today? One who might have glowing red cheeks? *Literally* glowing? A somewhat full-figured woman with artificial purple eyes?"

"Artificial? Why, everything's artificial about all of us! Even you!" She laughs at the notion. "Unless we care to walk about wearing absolutely nothing, we are always lying to the outer world about what we're truly made of. In fact, I dare argue that we make no less than a hundred different efforts a day at hiding precisely what we are from others. Oh," she sings with a sad shake of her head, "if the others only knew how insecure I am about the fleshy bags upon my hips, or that I desperately wished I had a little forever-daughter named Geneva whose hair I could braid, or that my one true desire is to be owned and ravished by the lovely and handsome man named—Oh, but now I'm telling you too much!"

And not telling me enough. "So, have you seen her?"

"Oh, a woman with purple eyes and glowing cheeks? No, I'm afraid not," the woman confesses, stepping over the skinny trunk of a fallen tree as we walk.

The news weighs heavily upon me. The rest of the trip through the woods is filled with more and more of the woman's endless chatter. She tells me all the most important things I need to know about this city we're traveling to, a city called After's Hold with tons and tons of merrily-living men, women, and children. I miss about ninety-seven percent of what she's said, far too distracted with the fact that Mari is still out there somewhere, lost.

But the pale boy said she's alive. Was that a sweet lie meant to pacify me, or was it true? If that's the case, then he is the only one who can help me find her.

The fog gives way to tall metal walls quite abruptly. With it being so dark and hazy, I had no warning that we were approaching our destination at all. "Here are the gates of the great city of After's Hold," the woman says, presenting them. The great ugly things creak as they slide apart, revealing a long road lined with buildings and storefronts vanishing in the infinite distance.

We enter the great city, collectively startled by the change in scenery from the gloomy woods. The streets are paved like those in the countryside, not metal-plated as the university's are. They are cracked, too, and hugged by the likes of tall, daunting buildings that seem to stare down at us as we pass. The woman talks on and on, introducing each building as we go, but I don't pay her much attention, too overly stimulated by the sights. Did the Dead build this city, or is it a great, stony relic from the past that still stands? Most of the buildings are made of brick and wood, and many of the windows are missing, which creates a curious aural effect as the wind blows and snakes in and out of them. Judging from the darkness of them, I have to presume there's no electricity here. I wonder if they even have running water, what with their being dead and terrified of it and all.

"And just down that road, you'll find the park! One of many, in fact, though I fear it will be considerably less *green* than the ones you're used to. Oh, and over here, you'll find a row of abandoned buildings that once served a purpose. They're quite fun to stroll about in, if you're feeling *curious*. Down this way, you'll see—"

Really, she could be telling me the secret to life and I'll

miss every word. Somewhere down the street, I spot two others strolling along. Are they Living or Dead? I can't tell. By the window of a store with a large dark blue awning, there's a quaint group of three peering inside and commenting to one another, a small child among them arguing about a toy she wants.

"Don't mind them," says the woman quietly as we pass a cobblestone courtyard where a circle of Dead sit at a table, their game of cards interrupted as they stop to watch us. "They're just staring at you because of all that loud noise you're making in your chests."

I bring a protective hand up to my heart, yet again.

"You must be quite exhausted," murmurs the woman as we happen on a large, paved plaza lined with what appear to be various hotels and apartment buildings, if I had to guess. "We have countless places for you to rest your handsome, strapping Heart Beater heads," she says, her eyes landing on John, and not so subtly. "Do you prefer the Courtland Condos down that way, my sleepy Livings? Or maybe the Hildaberry Hotel & Spa back from where we'd come? Or perhaps the Moonrise? Escobar's Eatery & Bed? The apartment complex on 5th, the apartment complex on 6th, the apartment—well, there's complexes all the way up to 40th, really, but so many of them are empty—or would you like to try—?"

"That one," I say, pointing to the building nearest us.

Everyone turns their attention to the building that so drew mine. It's a warped, strange-looking thing, half its bricks appearing red, the other half an offish grey. There is a sickly, leafless tree in its courtyard, its thorny branches seeming to reach for us.

"No," the woman says sadly. "No, you won't want to stay there."

"Why not?"

"It's a cursed place. Not even the Dead will occupy its rooms. Really, I can recommend twenty other places that are far, far more suitable for—"

"We'll stay there," I insist, growing more adamant the more this woman protests.

Dana comes to my side. "Don't disturb the spirits any more than you already have," she warns me. "I would heed the warning from a person who knows—"

"You heed warnings from *crystal balls*," I spit back, annoyed at Dana's unsolicited advice.

"Why do they say it's cursed?" asks John, coming forth. East stands at his side, nearly joined to his hip as if John had become his almighty protector.

The strange woman faces John with pleasure, smiling at him longingly. Then, she shakes her head. "Oh, my handsome Human, it's a sad, sad story. Too long to tell, too old to truly know. It's said that a great green flame swallowed this building from its foot to its crown," she tells us, her voice wriggling with dramatic air. "I can't fathom what would make a flame *green*, but it is not a sight I care to envision. Years later, the half that'd burned was rebuilt. Still, no one dares. Haunted, they say. Haunted!" The woman laughs suddenly. "The Undead! Calling it haunted! Can you imagine?"

"We'll stay there," I decide.

I ignore the baffled stares from my companions. Don't they see the benefit in staying somewhere that even the Dead are afraid of? We'll be safe. Superstition itself will protect us from the prying eyes of the Dead—or the other Living. Besides, I'm secretly wondering if this building has made the Histories, creeping into my notes somewhere.

"The Winter's Retreat it is, then," says the woman with a halfhearted moan and a flick of her wrist. "Please, make your way. I fear I won't follow you too far in."

John and I share a look, then I lead the way through the courtyard hugged by the calmly reaching trees. East and Dana draw behind us close as can be. I feel the tension between John and I, even despite our unusual circumstance. I'm certain he still feels the sting of my slap across his face, which I felt was deserved. The words he uttered still repeat over and over in my head like a pair of goldfish circling a bowl, their tiny little world, passing by that same plastic rock formation a hundred times.

When we step through the creaky doors of the so-named Winter's Retreat, the woman holds open the double doors and allows us into the lobby, which I'm rather surprised to say is quite well-kept despite its lack of light and haunting reputation. Maybe the ghosts here were all expert housekeepers in their past life?

The smell reminds me of a lodge my parents took me to when I was only ten or so, a lodge in the snowy north. I remember the smoke and the fire, and the crisped chunks of meats we ate off the ends of sticks, and all the sweets. None of it made me enjoy the winter setting; I *hated* the cold and secretly dreaded the trip. Maybe that place was called Winter's Retreat, too. Long after my mom had gone to sleep, my dad stayed up with me by the fire and shared stories of his youth and how *his* father used to take him fishing in the ice lakes. *"Almost fell in the hole,"* he'd said with a hearty laugh. *"Imagine if I had? Oh, the cold there was so merciless, you felt like your very bones were collecting ice. But the fish we caught, oh, the tastiest I've ever known! Mm, and the memories we made! He died soon after, as I told you before. Pity you never met him."* His light eyes connected with my little child ones. *"Lesson I learned that day is, you must suffer for your joys, Jennifer. There is no happiness in the world without the suffering it takes to attain it."* He knew I hated the winter and the trip, and I think that speech of his was meant to settle somewhere in my heart. Strange, how I've disregarded his advice all my life

… until now, in this very moment. *You must suffer for your joys, Jennifer …*

"Yes," whispers Dana at my back. "Yes, yes, yes. I feel the spiritual essence so strongly here. A cold essence. There is much pain in this place. There is much regret."

"There is much bullshit dropping out of your mouth," I retort just as quietly.

"I will be just down the street," the woman declares with another demonstrative sweep of her hands. "There are at least ten rooms per floor, and you are welcome to stay in whichever you please. Mind the spiders; there may be a legion or two. Oh!" The woman slaps herself in the head. "I've not even bothered with the courtesy of names! Please forgive me! I am Truce. What may I call you?" Her eyes rest on John, likely only caring for *his* name.

"*Lucky*," sings the diviner gaily, matching the Truce lady's weirdness and flair. "That is what we are. Oh, and grateful for your hospitality, too. And we are also—"

"Jennifer," I volunteer, interrupting the diviner's farce. "This is East. She is Dana. And he is John. And," I add with a pang of hurt, "should you come across a woman with purple eyes and red, faintly-glowing cheeks—that's *literally* glowing, not just figuratively speaking—her name is Marianne, and I am her friend who desperately wants to know she's alright."

"Oh." Truce brings a hand to her lips, pain entering

her eyes. "I am so sorry to hear. I do hope your friend is found by us first, and not the savages."

I cringe at those words, then take a step forward. "What will you do with him?" I ask. "The boy you found with us? The … *savage*? Will you interrogate him?"

"What for? They are Undead-gone-wrong. Corrupted and forever bloodthirsty. Broken beyond our wildest hope of repair. Nothing can be done for him."

Wait. Does she mean …? "You're executing him?"

"No, my Jennifer. The Undead cannot die, of course!" The woman's golden curls jiggle as she chuckles. "Please do not worry about the boy. He will be taken care of."

Taken care of. I very much dislike the tone of those words. "But we need him," I insist. "He knows where my friend is. He's the last one who saw her."

Truce's expression grants me no comfort. I can see her suspecting the reason the boy was the last to see my friend is because he ate her, and I like that not at all.

"I'm sorry," she offers. "Truly and really and certainly sorry. I will tell the watchmen all about your friend and we will keep every Undead eye open for her, should she appear in our vicinity." She dramatically sighs with relief, as if considering the issue with my friend entirely handled by those useless words. "Now, my dears, you can rest! In this … scary, forsaken structure," she adds with a wince. "Any*who*, when you wish to see the rest of the city, simply find me down the street if you'd like a guide. It is quite a large city, I do declare! Wouldn't want you to get lost." Her eyes nervously scan John again, a giggle getting stuck in her throat. "So handsome. I may even still be down the street when you wake! All the local Dead relax there and socialize. Oh, to have actual guests in Winter's Retreat! Guests that *sleep!* What a curiosity! We haven't had a single guest here since …" Her voice trails off, lost in a thought that grows darker the longer she's lost in it.

"We are so very fortunate for your hospitality," Dana offers in the silence, bringing Truce's attention back. "It is a wonderfully generous thing you've done, putting a roof over our weary heads, and troubling the spirits for a bed upon which to lay our faces. Might I inquire," she goes on, her airy voice annoyingly melodic, "where in this great city we might find some Heart Beater sustenance?"

Truce wrinkles her face. "Sustenance?"

"Food," I blurt out, my patience lost. "People food. Something to eat. Water."

"Oh! Yes, of course," Truce agrees. "Down the street as well. There is a lovely restaurant, though I fear I know little about it. You could perhaps ask the other Livings, yes? Ah, but I know there is a building with *water* that's drawn from the ground, though I'm afraid nothing runs in the pipes. Forgive me for my gross and unforgiveable ignorance on the matter; I haven't had to worry about such things in a lifetime. The others here with noisy chests stay at a lodge just up the street, two blocks. It's but a short minute or two's stroll that way," she explains, pointing. "Maybe you wish to stay in their lodge instead?"

"No," I answer quickly before Dana says anything stupid. "We're quite fine where we are. Thank you for your kindness, Truce."

"Of course, of course. Oh, to be alive again. Are you two … Are you two a couple?" she asks, pointing at John and I. "So sweet, young Living love," she murmurs with a tinge of sadness before we even have a chance to answer. "So handsome. So strapping and *flushed* and … just, oh." Truce spreads her lips into a big curly smile, admiring us as if we were made of gold and glitter. "You bring great joy to my unbeating heart, you sweet noisemakers. Please stay here forever!" Then, with a little waltz, she vacates the lobby, the door shutting gently behind her.

I face the others. "We're among them now. The *real* Beautiful Dead. These are the Undead we came here to see, not the ones who nearly ate us at the hovercraft."

"We can't be so quick to trust."

I look at John, the one who just spoke. I still hurt when I look at him, but I'm not sure anymore if it's just because of what he said in the woods, or something else entirely. What the hell is wrong with me?

"We may have been welcomed," he goes on, "but we

can't trust anyone but ourselves." His warm brown eyes glow in the dim light coming in through the window, the sight of which warms me instantly. I hate that I notice this when I'm supposed to be angry with him. "At least not yet. We have your satchel of food," he adds, giving eyes to a wary East, "and it's from that satchel that we should maintain ourselves while we stay in our room."

"Room? One room?" Dana looks between us, her eyes alight with puzzlement. "But there are countless from which to choose. Why must we all—?"

"Stay together?" John finishes. "Didn't I just say why?"

"Trust no one," she repeats, defeated.

His eyes graze mine longingly, waiting to see if I will raise any objection. I only offer him my cool silence, too many emotions still making artwork of my nervous system for me to trust anything I might rashly say.

"We will take turns with our rest," he announces. "We can't all be asleep when the Dead walk every hour of the days and nights long. Even if this Truce lady can be trusted, she certainly can't speak for the character of a hundred or more other Dead who live here. What if there are savages among them? What then? Should we look forward to waking up tomorrow morning with our throats missing, or our hearts pried from our chests?"

"John."

He looks at me, his eyes flashing with anticipation. He

wants me to forgive him, or to acknowledge him, or to say anything that would settle his worries. I regrettably find myself incapable of doing any of those things. "We will be fine in separate rooms. Surely the doors lock. If one of us must stand guard outside of them to keep our peace of mind, so be it, I'll take the first watch." Without waiting for a response, I make my way up the stairs.

The moment I enter number 209, I make my way to what I presume to be the attached bathroom, put myself inside it, shut the door, and explode into silent tears. I can't keep this up any longer. Between John's words that I know he didn't mean and the ones he did, and the ones I've been waiting for him to say since we met … I don't know what I'm so upset about anymore. I can't even think about poor Mari. I'm so far away from home, and the whole purpose of journeying to this strange land has already died in my chest. No excitement lives there anymore—just a whole bunch of *noise* that only the Dead can hear.

"Jennifer."

His voice is muffled through the door I'm leaning my back against. I sigh through the soundless tears I've let out. My face is probably a gross, snotty mess.

If Mari were here, she'd supply me the perfect colors and makeup to put my face to rights. *Are you sure you don't want Icecap Blue for your eyes?* she asked me once. *They complement your skin so much better.* I kept preferring Gaea's Navel because I loved the color of summertime and grass. Winter, not so much. I hate the cold. It reminds me of trips to the northern lodge and my dad joking about falling through his fishing hole and freezing. *I'm terrified of freezing.* Still, the next time Mari asked, I finally gave in and took the Icecap Blue. Compliments flooded in like rain in the gardens. Even a rigid icicle like Professor Praun did a double-take in class that first day I wore the icy eyes.

John tries again. "Can we talk?"

I don't sniffle. I don't want to give him any indication that I've been crying. I'm embarrassed suddenly by it. I hate crying. "Maybe in a bit," I respond gently. "I just need a moment in here."

I hear John shuffle on the other side of the door. Then, in a changed tone, he says, "Can *we* at least share a room? I know I've sort of ..." He clears his throat, then goes on. "I've been a burden on you. For many, many months. I've lived in your condo and eaten your food. Your roommate had to get used to me. I make a mess in the kitchen."

Is this just John securing his place in my condo, assuming we ever make it back home? Is this just another of his countless games to keep me on his side? I'm so filled with doubts, I can't even think logically anymore. Every one of my rash, spur-of-the-moment decisions is entirely motivated by gut and raw emotion. I doubt that's a smart or efficient way to operate. Surely I've made a choice or two that's helped secure our impending demise.

"I'll never be able to repay you for the kindness you've shown me," he murmurs through the door.

"You don't have to repay me for a thing," I mutter, feeling awful suddenly. I really should fix up my horrible face before he sees me. I stumble through the dark, making my way to the sink. I twist the handle. It squeaks. No water; I'm gently reminded by the abundant *nothing* that comes out of the faucet.

He runs a hand down the door. I hear it sliding softly down the bumpy wood. "I shouldn't have said that bit in the woods about your dad. That was wrong."

"You really don't need to apologize, John," I tell him, annoyed at the shakiness that comes through my voice from trying *not* to cry. Really, I don't have time for all these dumb emotions. "I know you didn't mean it."

"Well, in a sense I did," he says. "I meant … that I don't want you to *die*, Jennifer. I meant … I meant that I care too much about you. I … I *like* you."

I give a doleful glance at the mirror. A wet and scary version of my face stares back. I don't look pretty. I'm an ugly crier. I don't know if John has learned this about me yet, or if now is totally the wrong time for him to find out. Hell, *I* certainly wouldn't want to kiss this face.

"Please come out of the bathroom and talk to me."

I use a sleeve to wipe my eyes as best as I can. I know it does little for me, if anything at all. I take a breath, then pull open the door. John and his chiseled, strong face and his infinite brown eyes and his short, messed-up hair and his thick shoulders greet me all at once. In this instant, I realize I miss him horribly and I don't want to be at odds with him for a second longer.

He doesn't move to hug me or anything. John's never been the lovey type. I've known that would be an obstacle for us; he reveals so little about what he feels inside that, when he finally does, it pulls the floor out from under me.

I think it pulls it out from under him, too. He doesn't seem to know what to say, now that he's got me out of hiding, so I offer the first words. "The others?"

"The delivery boy's across the hall. The seer is next to him. No sign of ghosts or … haunted things." He moves to the bed, gives it a pat. The sheet coughs out a cloud of dust, all the clumpy ashen flakes floating off to new homes. It's likely the first time anyone's disturbed them in a century, give or take. "Well, we could sleep on the floor," he considers instead.

I rush up and slam myself into his firm body to plant my lips upon his, catching poor, ever-stoic John off-guard. He turns into stone but for his mouth, which works a spell and a half on mine.

When the kiss ends, he tries to ask what I'm doing,

but I make him swallow the words with another sudden, forceful kiss. His mood changes, all pretense dropped, and quite suddenly it is the both of us competing to see who's the stronger kisser. Our hands join the competition, running up and down our sides and tugging on each other's tattered clothes.

He might be using me. He might be no good for me. I shouldn't want him, but damn it, I do.

I pull too hard. His dirty shirt rips. Neither of us care, because in the next instant it's on the floor. Then so are we, and the Sunless Reach and all its due worries and fears are long forgotten for hours, traded for emotions far more kind and preferable.

The next time my eyes open, I'm cradled in his big arms, my head against his bare chest, and the room is notably darker. Have we slept to the following evening, or was it never quite nighttime to begin with? My sense of time has been so altered in this creepy realm that I cannot even say, with confidence, how many days we've been here. Only one? Two days, yet? It feels like a lifetime.

I rise and slip out of the room, not wanting to disturb John. No, I don't learn my lessons. For the second time, I leave John sleeping, and I descend the stairs to the lobby of Winter's Retreat, then sit on the first step and stare at the front glass door and the darkness beyond it.

The rough floor definitely did a number on my back; I

wince as I nurse it as best as I can. I'm not used to sleeping on rough, wooden floors. So pampered I am, a Living from the land across the *ocean*. I smile, hearing Truce's voice saying that word again. I think I may come to like her, if she gives me a chance to ask about twenty or thirty more questions regarding her *death*ness.

I pull out the device from my pocket. I know John said to conserve its battery, but I need to know if it holds a key I've yet to consider in our journey. Within it are all my notes, all my conclusions ... and a legion of unanswered questions. Maybe some mention of a green flame might be lodged somewhere in my forgotten scribblings.

When I tap my fingers on it, the device does not respond. *The river,* I realize. *My device was completely submerged.* Panic makes a home in my nerves as I turn the device over and over in my hand, inspecting it with swelling frustration. I know the thing's suffered a bit of rain before; it ought to survive a brief plunge into dirty, deathly, thousand-year-old water, shouldn't it?

Finally—and tiredly—the screen emits a faint light, and then my notes appear before me. *Oh, thank you.* I do realize I may be compromising my device by waking it up and pushing through my notes, but I can't let this whole journey be a waste. I need to consult my digital brain. As I scroll through glitching, stuttering pages on the cranky device, I wonder if all my life I have unknowingly been preparing for this adventure. I ought to be the expert among us, yet I feel so out of place. I've never before appreciated more the vast and incomparable difference between learning a thing and *living* a thing. Ten years poring over History and Mythology books at the university couldn't prepare me for this.

Another digital page turns. I read: *Crazy Lady Number Five. Her name is Dana. She smells like cat pee.* I chuckle, but it dies quickly as thoughts of my father grip me tightly by the throat. Did Dana really see my father's spirit, or was it all a complete coincidence? Do spirits even exist? Funny I ask that, sitting here in the lobby of a so-called haunted building burned down by some mystery green fire.

I swipe the page again, continuing on. I skim words I've read a hundred times. I swipe quickly past notes I've written months ago, years ago, hurrying before my device decides that it's drowned. I wade through Histories and Mythologies, combing for all traces of my Beautiful Dead. I know there's something in here that will help me.

Professor Praun's voice seeps into my brain like a ghost, condemning me for my foolish actions. I can see him welcoming me back to the school with a cold stare and bearing an official notice of expulsion. Then, I see the authorities waiting for me at the edge of campus, ready to whisk me away to a prison somewhere.

"Don't you worry," I tell the imaginary professor and

authorities in my daydream. "When we come back, we'll have with us evidence that will change the world as we know it. I will justify my crimes. I'll be the last one laughing," I tell Praun especially.

"It is always good to laugh."

I twist my torso, catching sight of Dana descending the stairs as quietly as a cat. She whips past me like a breeze, waltzing across the lobby and casting shadows from the moonlight outside.

"It lets the spirits know you are not afraid," the diviner explains, dancing by the bar and tapping her fingers on each of the barstools, as if each one were a dance partner.

I scowl. "Why did you follow us onto the hovercraft? You never explained."

She comes to a sudden and dramatic stop, leaning her back against the bar, and says, "You were to *defame* me."

I squint at her. "What?"

"With your *article*." Now it's her turn to scowl, and I hear the hint of anger that so fueled her voice when she screamed at me as I left her house. That moment feels like so long ago. "You were going to tell the world that I was a fake. You had tricked me with that *lie* of your father. You made a fool of me, evil girl. I followed you back to the campus and I waited and I *watched* you. I planned to have a word, but ..." Her eyes drift somewhere, a dark thought clouding her expression. "I couldn't speak up. I wouldn't know what to say. I felt … I thought … I'd …"

"You thought I'd write an article calling you a fraud to the whole university?" I ask acidly.

"I ADMIT THAT IT MIGHT BE FAKE!" she shouts, all that joy she had just a moment ago shattering to the floor like a pretty glass vase. "The spirits! The mists! The summoning! It might all be *fake*," she goes on, her voice terse and pointed, her eyes flashing, "but *the healing is real!* I look upon people's mourning, their grief-stricken eyes, and I see a *need* for my service, a *need*. I summon the spirits of the deceased and I tell the survived what they *need* to hear to get the closure they *deserve*. Oh, if only someone could have done that for me when I lost my husband and little girl. It's a miracle from the beyond that I still stand here in the middle of *Death's home itself*, and I'm still breathing."

I've gotten to my feet, clutching the device to my stomach and watching Dana's eyes roll as she fights her own emotional outburst. I have a sudden urge to rush up and hug her. I have another urge to bludgeon her over the head with my shoe. I think maybe I was ready to hate her the moment I entered that house, equipped with my lie.

My lie, which not hours later became true.

"I had no intention of defaming you," I tell her. "I'm sorry if you felt deceived, but with all due respect, your entire business is in deception. You were bound to get served your own medicine at some point, Dana."

To that, she huffs, then paces in a circle around the lobby, shaking her head and seeming to sift through a million thoughts a second. I can't imagine what's in that lunatic's head; I can only assume it's crowded in there.

She stops suddenly. "Your friend." She lifts her eyes but doesn't quite meet mine. "I do not sense her."

I frown. "What do you mean?"

"I do not sense her spirit in the mists, no matter how hazy they are lately. Do you understand my meaning?" Now, Dana's eyes find mine. "She is not yet deceased."

I stare at her, wondering if I'm being served the very medicine I just accused her of serving. Does she mean to simply put my mind at ease with a well-intended lie? Or is there something real about this woman's power?

I clear my throat. "If only you were skilled in sensing the *Living*," I remark with a subtle smile, "then perhaps you'd be useful in seeking her out."

Encouraged, Dana returns my expression with a tiny smile of her own. "I am so very useless."

"Worst diviner ever," I agree.

The scraping of shoes make me spin, finding John and East at the top of the stairs, drawn most likely by her prior outburst. John still wears no shirt, his jeans hanging loose on his hips, torn at the knees. East's uniform, hilariously soiled beyond recognition, is unbuttoned and untucked, showing a sliver of his undershirt beneath in the way that storm clouds part to reveal a blinding sky.

I sigh with relief. "Mari's alive."

John comes down the stairs quickly and noisily. "You found her? How?"

"No." I give a nod at the diviner. "She can't sense her spirit. That means Mari has not died. That means Mari is out there and her joyous heart is beating, beating, beating. I, for one, am quite comforted by that news." I hug my device and close my eyes, feeling the peace.

"Really?" says John as dryly as the wood beneath our shoes. "Is this some sort of joke?"

"No joke. We're going to explore this town and get all the information I need. I want to learn every last thing I can from these people. *My* people." I give my device a wiggle, then stash it back in my pocket.

"So the crazy-hair lies to you," John goes on, "makes up some crap about your friend's spirit—*our* friend—and you accept it? A bunch of empty, consoling words?"

"Yes." I give him a knowing look. "So I better gather as much intel as I can before, y'know, *our rescue crew comes and saves us*," I say, tossing John's sugar-coated lie right back at him. Then, with a dainty twist of my heel, I push through the glass doors and into the night.

Chapter Five

The Broken Road Of Destiny

Though the city of After's Hold is four times the size of my university, judging from what Truce and a pair of her odd friends describe to us, the entire population only occupies the mere space of four quaint city blocks. Truce says that a friend or two of hers will rarely explore the other areas of After's Hold, which are otherwise entirely abandoned. The city is so vast and empty and lonesome, its farthest corners and crumbling buildings so wretched from the history and secrets it keeps, that most Dead have grown superstitious and fearful of it.

Imagine that.

Already, we've made the other Dead nervous with our choice in residence. I guess that's my fault. "I heard of a girl with white hair," murmurs an Undead lady with slimy eyes that have no pupils. "Like yours," she teases, reaching a hand out to touch my hair, "and she was the unluckiest, cruelest, saddest girl who ever unlived."

"Yes," I say, having heard about the girl before, "but

what does that have to do with Winter's Retreat?"

"No idea," she murmurs sadly.

I learn that, contrary to what's written over and over again in the Histories, the Dead eat and drink nothing. The wild creatures of the woods, including that pale boy who is certainly destroyed by now, are the only ones of them who feed on Living people and animals, but it is not known why.

"They're just bored," says a wiry old man with a grey goatee that hangs down to his chest. "Bored and looking for new things to do to entertain themselves. Like drink blood. Eternity is awful boring."

"Awful boring," agrees Truce. "Ooh! Let's show them the Broken Road of Destiny!"

The Broken Road of Destiny turns out to be the remnants of an ancient highway that stretches onward in broken fragments from the south exit of After's Hold. No one seems able to explain the meaning behind the overly dramatic title, but I'm assured that it's super deadly and nothing at all worth knowing lies in its direction. For some reason, I have a creeping suspicion that this, too, has to do with "the girl with white hair" and all the bad luck and curses associated with that unfortunate individual.

"Really inconvenient time to have long, white hair," remarks John in my ear. Color me a shade of not-amused.

I take so many notes on my glitch-ridden device that

my fingertips go numb. The Dead were once alive, like me, like John, like anyone, but some odd circumstance of nature and science and—magic?—brings them back for a Second Life. The trouble is, their First Lives were so long ago that none of them seem interested at all in talking about them, regardless of my mounting curiosity. I think Marianne could provide better insight as to the science of their strange reanimation, seeing as the dead definitely do not rise on our side of the world.

At least, not yet.

The Dead never sleep, not even for a second. Their entire existence is one long, eternal day. Their entire existence is freedom. It's us unfortunate Living who are still caught in the almighty *trap* of hunger, thirst, and weariness ... a never-ending cycle.

"But you make entertaining sounds in your chests!" Truce exclaims merrily, but of course she's made that point before. It almost doesn't get old.

There are conflicting stories about where the Dead come from, or what exactly keeps them half-alive. Some believe they *are* alive, but simply in a different way. Then there are some who believe in some eternal energy called Vita, or Planet's Blood, or Anima.

It's to that last word, Anima, that John gives a nod of recognition, as he'd heard the term before. I had to look it up a term or two ago when John first mentioned it and, strangely, its history has no connection with the Dead at all. In fact, the only place I found it written was in an old children's storybook about six wise men and women who had eyes that glowed green and yellow and winter white. The story was a silly tale about why people have happy and sad feelings, and it involved something about the white and yellow lights always battling the green.

It was the green light that was called "Anima".

When an opportune moment in a conversation lets Dana take the spotlight and ask her own questions about the ever-elusive spirit world and what strange twist of Anima has granted her this "immortal gift of sight", a large Undead man with a chin as big as his forehead leans in to say, "Might be some truth to your claim. Legend has it, there once lived special people who could give life, take life, and manipulate the will o' the Dead."

They had many names, she was told. Necromancers. Spiritkeepers. Warlocks.

"Spiritkeeper," Dana decides right then. "Yes! I much prefer that term. Oh, if my name could be Spana ... Yes, Spana the Spiritkeeper. Oh, but it could still be!" I watch as the dollar signs glow in her irises and she imagines the name printed on every publication in the world.

Not all of the Dead are so friendly to us *breathers*. After Truce makes a joke about nail colors in the shaded patio of a restaurant on 43rd Avenue and inspiring the whole of us to laugh, I notice a woman seated in the shadows by the wall, her face hidden under the dramatic black brim of a hat twice the size of a dinner plate. Even in the shadow that her headpiece casts, I see the glint of bitterness in her eyes and the resentment that lives and dies on the curling of her white, bloodless lips. Her pasty legs are crossed, her hands curled in the lap of her black dress that cuts off at the knee, hugging her slender form. She sits there and watches, unimpressed and unmoved.

No, I don't skip over to her table to introduce myself.

It's roughly five hours into our day—or is it night?—when we finally meet the other Livings. Three of them hide out in a room above one of the restaurants, and the other two stay across the street at the top of a brick tower called the Weston, as is indicated by the dilapidated oaken sign that hangs above its entrance. Yes, that's *five* Livings, not the ten or twenty that Truce earlier claimed.

The two at the top of the tower care to see no one but themselves, keeping far away. We're left to just assume they exist at all. Not so social, apparently.

Neither are the three Livings we *do* meet. One of them, a dark-skinned woman with jagged locks of hair that look like they were taken to by a two-year-old with scissors, leads the trio. Her sunken eyes regard me like I were the most annoying thing to happen to her day.

"What're you here for?" she demands before even a

proper hello.

I glance at the other two behind her: a sickly boy with orange hair and freckled yellow skin who couldn't be older than twelve, and a stark, bronzed man with dark hair to his shoulders who matches John for his muscles, but looks like he's got a vacancy or two in his brain attic.

"For … educational purposes," I answer, unsure the angle of her question, "though we hadn't intended to strand ourselves here. At least, not exactly." I extend a hand to her. "I'm Jennifer."

"I'm sure you are," she returns coolly, ignoring my extended hand, her dark eyes narrowing.

I glance at John. These people don't trust us. I guess that should be expected. "What brought you here?" I ask, dropping my hand. These people aren't the scientists or researchers I was hoping for them to be.

She lifts her chin, her jagged sprouts of hair bobbing in reaction. "My innocence got me here," she answers.

"Your … innocence?"

She takes one step forward. "I'll make myself perfectly plain, *Jennifer*." Her hardened gaze runs over me, from my eyes, to my toes, and back. "You and your friends keep to your haunted little waste of a building, and the three of us will keep to ours. The waterworks," she adds with a cold nod in a certain direction, "is neutral ground. You get the water you need, then you get back to your little burned-down hole."

Taken aback by her brashness as I may be, I stand my ground and refuse to cower. "Why are you treating us like this? We're alive, like you," I say, as if it's necessary to point it out. "We're … kin. Shouldn't we work together?"

"You're another mouth that needs wetted, another belly that needs filled." The way she says it, it sounds like half an accusation. "If I see you so much as *breathe* on our home, I'll open your neck with my switchblade, then cut that pretty white hair of yours off and make a bow out of it for my violin." Still as a statue, the girl's dark eyes flick to the left, regarding John for a solid moment, then Dana, then a quivering East. "Do you like music? I like music. I bet your hair will make the sweetest song to my friends' hungry, Human ears. And your blood will make a sweeter one to these vile, hungry Dead, who will lap up every last drop." She smirks. "Don't fool yourselves. We're all just counting days here in the land of the Dead. Better you count yours on your own."

With that, she gives a snap to her two friends, then slips back into their restaurant—which I guess we ought to regard as their *totally-off-limits turf*—and when the door slams, it slams with the dreaded bang of a judge's gavel.

"A friendly bunch," I remark. "Maybe I should have invited them over for tea."

"We don't have any tea," says East miserably. "You

can take on the big guy, can't you, John?" John regards his question with a baleful glare. "Sorry. I just thought—"

"In a land with few potential companions among the quavering, sleepless spirits, we oughtn't offend those we could befriend," reasons the ever earthbound Dana. Note my drooling sarcasm—practically drowning in it.

"They're just protecting their own," I say, staring at the door of the restaurant. "It's reasonable. They see us as a threat. They think we'll steal their food, or …" I study the windows of the building, considering whether that deadly trio is watching us right now. "I suppose we might be the same as them, if we had little."

"We have little," states East.

Later, we return to our haunted little dwelling with four modest buckets of water with which to wash and drink. From the satchel, we draw a tiny bit of dinner for each of us. I'm suddenly abundantly thankful for East's burst of bravery before we abandoned our ship. Oh, to imagine how much food is still on that ship. *If only we could sneak back to it … If only we could gather four or five more satchels' worth …* Even after we've eaten, we are all so clearly unsatisfied and still hungry, though none of us voice our whiny, Humanly complaints.

"We learned a lot today," says John after East and Dana have gone upstairs to sleep.

I lean my back against him, glad to feel his arms

tighten around me in response. Yet, for all the answers I've gained today, I still have the one painful question that remains unanswered: where the hell is my friend? Here I am, whining about my hunger, and Mari likely hasn't eaten anything for days. I feel guilty even for the little bit I've let myself enjoy.

"We'll learn more tomorrow," I reply despondently.

"We need to unite with the others somehow."

"Really? The one that wants to make a violin bow out of my hair?" I snort derisively. "Nothing good's going to come from them. What we *really* need to do is figure out how they're surviving, where they're getting their food. Truce said the restaurants have some, and this city is enormous. Maybe there's more of it elsewhere. Surely the three of them aren't occupying the *only* food source here."

"What kind of food could possibly exist in a thousand-year-old city?"

"They're alive, aren't they? Maybe there's a garden."

"There's the two others living in that brick tower, the Weston," he reminds me. "Maybe they're friendlier."

"Maybe they're deadlier," I shoot back.

He squeezes me in his arms. "We can explore a bit tomorrow," John whispers into my ear. "We'll figure out where we can get—"

"I need to find Mari. I need to find her *yesterday*."

He sighs in my ear. "I know."

"And you know who will help us."

"No." John shifts, twisting himself so he can see my face. "No, we're not seeing that—that creature. Besides, he's probably … *really* dead by now. Actual dead."

"He's our only hope. I'll feel so much better if the *five* of us were all here, John. Then at least we'd be miserable *together.*" I stare at the window. "She's out there."

His stomach growls, filling the room with its agony. Mine shares the same. "What do you propose we do?"

I climb to my feet, determined. "East and Dana can rest. I don't trust harm will find them here. I need to find Corpsey and—"

"Corpsey? Oh, right. Your name for … *him*. Jennifer, please don't." John's on his feet too, and he comes around to meet my eyes. I hate how persuasive his deep brown irises can be, set in that rough, sexy face of his. "We can head out of After's Hold tomorrow, first thing. We'll head back over the river if we have to. We'll find her, but please don't go to that creature. I don't trust him."

"Thing is," I say quietly, "I think *he* trusts *me*."

"What do you mean?"

Before I can explain it, I'm heading out the door. John follows, hissing his protests at me, but I don't listen. I push through the eerie darkness of the streets, trying my best to ignore how unnerving it is to walk the streets of an enormous city that has a population of less than twenty. I feel every reservation bubbling inside me like some toxic potion in my belly, threatening to toss up the tiny bite I just had for "dinner", but I've set my mind and I force myself to keep throwing one foot in front of the other.

Truce is precisely where I expect her to be. She turns at the sight of me and her creepy eyes flash with joy—or maybe it's just because John is with me too. "My pretty! My handsome! Ah, is it morning already? How time flies." She chortles. "Want to visit Reilly's Furniture on 9th?"

"Actually, I'd like to visit something else. Some*one,*" I amend. "I know you strictly forbade it, but—"

"Nothing is 'strictly forbade' in After's Hold!" she exclaims happily. "Except for drinking blood. That vile act is most certainly forbade. Forbid? Forbidden? What a strange word." She smacks her lips, confused.

"I want to see the savage boy."

Truce's face loses all merriment in the space of one second. She turns her gaze on me, her expression growing troubled. "Oh, sweet Living Jennifer, how you *test* me."

"I don't mean to test anything," I assure her. "I just need to see him. I know he's doomed to be destroyed or ended or whatever, but I—"

"Not ended, no."

I share a glance with John, my eyebrows lifting, then turn back to her in surprise. "So he's still alive?"

"*Un*alive, yes," she agrees with a tinge of regret in her

voice. "The Mayor decided to let him *blood* a bit before … handling him," she explains delicately. "I cannot fathom why, but the Mayor now and then decides to take heart with the wild ones and study what happens when they are deprived of their *snack* for some time. She's convinced they can turn back to normal. I fear she's clinging to a silly hope; the boy is too far-gone."

"Mayor, you said?"

"Yes. I'm afraid you must request an audience with the boy through the Mayor. The savage boy's being kept in a room in her office for safety." Truce draws close to me—too close—and puts a puffy hand on my shoulder. "My dear Jenny-thing, it is always an Undead's duty to let go of their past. I have gained and lost so many friends along the course of time, and—"

"No!" I pull away from her at once, nearly backing into John. "I'm not giving up on my friend. I refuse to. Don't even suggest it. She's out there!" I insist. "I just need to find out where, and then I need to get her back."

Truce sighs gently, then nods, giving in. "Very well. Come. I will take you to Mayor Damnation."

It isn't a joke. The Mayor's name for this Second Life of hers is actually Damnation. Most prefer to simply call her Mayor, or just plain Damn. No, I don't understand it either. I don't have the guts to ask if the name is meant in humor—or if she meant *Dame* and got confused, perhaps?

Nonetheless, I'm escorted down the throat of a long building and brought into the office of Mayor Damnation herself. She sits on a throne made of overturned filing cabinets, thick books, and shredded paper. She's reading when we enter the room, her legs dangling off the pile of knowledge. She's dressed in a totally unremarkable blue robe—the kind that might be provided to you by a cheap hotel. Her hair is fuzzy and white, giving her head the appearance of the end of a cotton swab. Judging from her wrinkled skin, I'd put her at about an approximate Human age of seventy or more, despite her being Dead. As soon as we enter, she looks up from her book and blinks twice. Her startlingly crimson eyelashes are ghastly long, two inches at least. I'm sure she uses them to catch flies and fan her own cheeks on a hot summer day.

"Are these our new Livings?" asks the Mayor. Her voice is surprisingly high and melodic, far sweeter and more inviting than I anticipated. She reminds me of my grandmother on my mom's side of the family. I can already smell the holiday cookies baking in the oven. My stomach growls; that was a cruel thing for my mind to do.

"This one's named Jenny-thing. Oh, sorry." Truce clears her throat. "Jenni*fer* is her name. The strapping, beefy, dashing, handsome young male next to her is *John*." Truce wiggles her eyebrows at him.

Mayor Damnation sets her book aside. It slides down

the pile of crap she sits on, completely forgotten, as she looks on the Living likes of us. "My, my. You're a good-looking pair of Humans," she says, her eyes brightening. "Healthy, the two of you. I heard there's two others as well? Another young fellow and a lady?"

"Connor and Dana," I confirm, "though Connor goes by East."

"I've always loved the east," she remarks. "It's a nice direction. The direction of impending morning."

I smile at her. "Thank you for letting us stay here in your city," I make sure to tell her, figuring starting things off on a *polite* foot would do us best.

"No thanks needed." The Mayor crosses her legs, the tired blue robe flapping in protest. "This city isn't really mine. I claim no ownership. Even half my own body isn't mine," she remarks with a throaty snicker. "Should've seen me when they pulled my sad ass out of the dirt. Ha! I was missing both my legs from the knee, down. My jaw, gone, and I had a serious bite taken out of my arm. Don't want to imagine what the hell the last few minutes of my First Life were like! I can't imagine I died laughing."

I tilt my head, curious. "You don't remember how you died? It was that long ago?"

"It's called a Waking Dream, honey-poo," she tells me as she rises from her seat, then stumbles down the pile of overturned furniture and paper. Wow, she's easily seven feet tall. I have to keep my mouth from gaping. "Think of it like a shot of memories," she says, "instantly recalling everything about your long, boring First Life in one fiery, horrific second. I have *not* had one of those."

"How does one go about having a Waking Dream?" I ask, wondering if it would be rude to pull out my device and take notes.

"They just happen. They have a mind of their own," she says, coming to a stop in front of us. I have to crane my neck upward to meet her gaze. "Or, in the case of my Waking Dream that's yet to come, it doesn't have a mind at all. How can I help you?"

To the point, at last. "I need to see your prisoner."

"Prisoner? Oh, right, the wildcat. Why?"

"He was the last to see my missing friend," I explain to her. "I'm hoping he knows more than he admitted last time we spoke."

"Oh? You actually got him to speak? Curious." The Mayor picks at her nails. "He wouldn't do a thing but growl at me. I was tempted to throw a stick and see if he'd retrieve it."

"Probably suck the blood out of it first," I remark. "Can I see him? Time is of the essence. My friend—"

"This way." The Mayor beckons, sauntering past us and out of the room. After shooting a glance at John, we follow the tall Damn woman down a hall, around a corner, up a set of stairs, and then through a door where she has to duck to make it inside.

The room is what I presume to be a generously-sized janitorial closet, or a room to keep police evidence, or a tiny pharmacy—I have no idea, as most of its contents have been emptied. Dividing the room in half is a line of metal bars like a cage, stretching from one wall to the other with a metal door interrupting it. *Makeshift-prison-cell* is a term that comes to mind.

On the other side of the bars sits Corpsey, our friendly pale boy. He's cross-legged on the bare, concrete floor, his hands resting in his lap. He looks up when we enter, his colorless eyes finding us. The only light in the room comes from a candle in the corner, and its flame casts a dancing shadow of the boy across the stark room.

"The only thing I ask," says the Mayor, "is that you keep on this side of the room and don't come too close to the bars where he can harm you—you both are delicious and he will *not* hesitate to help himself."

But he did *hesitate, back in the woods. Twice now, he's held back from making a meal of me.* "Yes," I say instead. "Thank you for this opportunity."

"And finally, don't let him out," the Mayor finishes. "Come see me when you're finished speaking with him. I have a book I must return to. I did leave it at quite an exciting part." The Mayor gives us each a nod, then faces our Corpsey friend. "Behave, you wildcat, you."

Damnation ducks on her way out of the room, Truce reluctantly following. With only John, myself, and the twisting shadow of the boy along the floor, the room grows eerily silent, as if John and I are its only occupants and the pale boy is nothing but an illusion.

Except he isn't. "Hello," I say, breaking the quiet. He still stares at me. I'm relieved to note that I don't see any dark and toothy viciousness in his eyes. "I'm sorry you're in here." I take one small step toward the cage. "I didn't know this would happen. Are you okay?"

John leans into me. "Jennifer, seriously? This *thing* tried to kill us."

I face John. "This *thing* also spared my life." I come right up to the cage, breaking Mayor Damnation's first rule already, and kneel down. "Let's be friends. Do you have a name, or should I keep calling you Corpsey? I heard they were not going to destroy you. They just want to see if you'll turn back to normal. Maybe your thirst for blood will … go away," I add with hope. "Wouldn't that be nice? They're giving you a chance to change."

"I'll never change."

His voice surprises me again, just like the first time I ever heard it. Maybe it's due to the clarity of his words in this little room, echoing hollowly off the brick walls.

"You don't want to change?"

"No," he murmurs gently.

I study him, eye-to-eye, grasping at that connection we shared in the forest. It's almost like I know him. I feel oddly drawn to him. Maybe I'm completely projecting my own feelings onto the boy, but something tells me he feels the same strange pull between us.

I clear my throat. "Want to see your sister again?"

That changes his face. He lifts his head, the whites of his eyes flashing, and his chapped lips part.

Yep, that got his attention. "I want to see my friend again," I go on. "Perhaps we can strike some sort of deal."

"No, Jennifer."

It's John interjecting again, coming up to my side and standing over me, his head shaking back and forth and his jaw setting tightly. His body eclipses half the candlelight, throwing the boy into darkness.

Respectfully, I ignore him, keeping my eyes on the now-dimmed face of our Dead, bloodthirsty friend. "You have to know where my friend Marianne is. You saw her. You even said she was still alive. You must know. Tell me, Corpsey, *tell me*, and I will do everything in my power to get you out of here."

"Jennifer!"

"Please, sweet pale boy," I plead, gripping the bars of the cage now. "You have to know my word is good."

The boy rises. So do I. Slowly, he comes forth to the

edge of the cage, and it takes every ounce of strength (and perhaps stupidity) in me to not back away. When he stops, we're nearly nose to nose. John has turned into a stone statue of tenseness next to me.

"Hair as white as winter ..." the boy murmurs so quietly I almost don't hear him.

"Please," I repeat. "Tell me where she is."

Then the boy says, "The Whispers."

I frown. "The what?"

"She will be at the Whispers. In the south. The place where it all began."

"Where *what* all began?"

The boy scuffs a foot against the ground, his fingers wiggling impatiently. John flinches, noticing, ready at any second to launch himself between us. I feel the heat of his tense breath against the side of my cheek.

"Let me out," says the boy, "and I'll take you there."

"I don't have the key."

"There is no key. The door is made of steel. I cannot touch it."

"Why can't you touch it?"

"Because I've tasted of blood," he says, which totally just opened up a whole other bucket of questions I doubt I'll get answers for. "Open the door and I will take you. If we go now, perhaps we won't be too late."

Before he even finishes his sentence, my hands are on

the door, working the handle. John grips my wrist, his eyes flashing wide. "Jennifer …"

"He won't harm me," I hiss at John. "Let go of me."

"You're making the wrong decision," he presses on. "I know Marianne is in danger, and I care about her too, but this is *not* how we find her. We can get to this whispering place ourselves. South, he said. We'll go down the Road of Destiny or whatever it's called."

"You can't go on your own," states the boy.

The two of us turn to him, my and John's hands still stuck on the handle of the metal door. "And why not?" asks John tersely.

"The Whispers is not a place for the Living," he replies in his clear, crisp, lofty voice. "You will walk in circles and circles around that cursed, Undeadly place, never finding it. For hours, for days, for a lifetime, you'll never step foot in the Whispers. No Living can find it alone. There are dark and ancient powers that keep it hidden." His soft, pale gaze moves to John. I daresay they carry a strange, twisted sympathy in them. "Only a Dead can take you to the heart of the land of the Dead."

"Then Truce will take us there," John insists. "Or our new friend, Damnation."

"They haven't left this city in decades," he returns calmly. "They don't know the wild as I know it."

"John …"

John's face twists with frustration. I know he doesn't have the same connection that I seem to have with the pale boy, but I'm not about to bet my friend's life on our confidence alone in finding a supposedly unfindable place. We're lost in a land of deathly magic and oddities that defy everything we know about science. How can I *not* trust this Undead person's word?

Slowly, I give in and turn the handle. Even with John's grip on my wrist, he does not hinder me further. Our hands united, we open the cage door.

The next instant, my device is in my other hand, and I lift it to the boy's face. The light from it flashes, painting his skin an eerie shade of bright blue, startling him.

"This object is from the land of the Living," I tell the boy calmly. "It's made of pure steel. If you double cross us or break your honor in any way, I will press it to your face so hard, you'll wear a permanent scar of it to your second grave. Do we have an understanding?"

He stares at the blinding device, but his eyes seem more curious than they do threatened.

"So colorful," he murmurs. "Like flames."

I squint at him. "What?"

"That's why they light candles," the boy tells me, still transfixed to my device as though it were the prettiest thing he'd ever seen. "Our eyes don't regard darkness in the same way your Living ones do, but they also don't regard light in the same way, either. Trust me, you've never seen color until you're Undead." He smiles, staring unblinkingly into the bright light.

"In your realm, we don't quite regard light in the same way, either," I note. "Days here are just a subtle change of brightness to the night. I have yet to see the sun through the fog, even here in the city where I thought we were free from its greedy cover."

"The further south we go, the worse it gets," he warns us quietly. "You've not yet seen the darkest of the land of the Dead. Not truly."

I don't know if his words are meant to scare me, but they do. "Let's go."

Carefully, I move aside, and the pale boy cooperates, stepping out of the cage. This would be the *second* rule I've broken of the gracious Mayor Damn's. Maybe third. I hope she's forgiving, considering my predicament. John leads the way down the hall, and I pick up the rear with my device brandished, the pale boy caught between us.

It's in another hallway that John stops us, making a slight detour to remove something off the wall. When he returns, he holds a long yellow tassel that might have come from a banner or artwork or something. "Bend," he orders the pale boy, then secures the tassel around the boy's neck, forming a noose. I stifle a protest I'm about to make, letting John have his moment of control. When the makeshift leash is attached and the pale boy lifts his head, John gives it a gentle tug. "Uncomfortable?"

"The Dead know nothing of comfort," he returns.

"Good."

With a great length of the tassel coiled about John's shoulder, he continues on his way out of the building through a different door from which we'd entered. I guess that's because it would *not* be in our best interest to run into Truce or the Mayor and have them observe our blunt betrayal of their trust. *We'll return the wildcat when we're finished,* I'd like to say, but considering my track record of returning things I've stolen, a guilty stab in my chest shuts me right up.

From the side door, we spill onto the street, relieved to find not a soul in sight.

"When we find your friend," the pale boy warns me, "she will not be the same. No Human walks the *true* land of the Dead and returns unchanged."

I swallow a pang of hurt. "And neither will we."

The three of us hurry away from the four city blocks where everyone resides, and towards the Broken Road of Destiny we go; I hope our actual destiny is anything but.

Chapter Six

Whispers

John looks up at the tree, considering it.

"Don't you dare," I warn him.

He glances back at our friend, Corpsey. He puts a hand to his own chin, drumming fingers along his jaw.

"Don't," I say again.

John addresses our friend, Corpsey. "Your kind really feel no discomfort at all?"

"No."

"And you don't breathe?"

"No."

John nods. "Very well."

With that, John tosses the tassel over the nearest branch, then pulls with all his might. Corpsey lifts off the ground as if he weighs nothing—that, or John is a lot stronger than I give him credit for. He gives it another great heave and a grunt, then secures the tassel around a neighboring tree, tying it off.

I sigh. "I can't believe you did that."

Corpsey dangles there lazily by the neck. I daresay he appears bored.

"Can't take chances," mutters John, returning to me. "We need our rest. We've been on our feet for hours."

"I'm fine," rasps the pale boy with a wave of his hand. *"Really,"* he assures me when I look unconvinced. *"Totally fine. Can't feel a thing."* His strangled voice sounds more gravelly than my Aunt Belinda's and she's been smoking since she was ten. *"I'm just greeeat."*

After staring sadly at the dangling Undead boy for a moment, I finally concede, lowering myself to the ground and leaning against John, who's found a nearby tree to lean against within view of our dangling friend.

I experience a wave of guilt that unrests every nerve I just steeled before leaving After's Hold. The wave of guilt turns into words. "We should've grabbed water," I say, turning my head slightly. I hope John hasn't already fallen asleep at my back; he looked so exhausted. "Or food. Or thought to wake the others to come with us. I was selfish not to include them."

"We left on an impulse," John reminds me, his words vibrating through his chest and into mine. "Don't blame yourself, Jen. Look." He takes my hand into his, fiddling gently with my fingers. "If that fussy roommate of yours survived this long, so can we. Right? Can you imagine how whiny she'd be by now if she were with us? 'Jen, where can we find a bagel store around here?'"

I try to smile, but even the muscles in my face grow heavier by the second. I can hardly keep my eyes open. "I know you're trying to cheer me up, but—"

"Just imagine the relief we'll feel when she's with us and we're returning to After's Hold together," he tells me. "Just imagine how you'll feel when this is all over with and we're back home. They'll celebrate us. Don't you hear all your peers cheering after you've presented your dissertation to the class? The Beautiful Dead …"

The dream he's lending me sends my mind into a new direction. The dissertation … Notoriety … Vindication … John's acceptance and support from the financial aid …

"John, what will happen when you *do* get accepted into the university?" I ask, looking down as he starts to massage each of my fingers, his hands feeling so strong against mine. "When you're an official student. When you … don't need to stay in our condominium anymore. What'll happen?"

His silence unsettles me. For a moment, my fears all along are confirmed. He'll move on when the university takes him in. He'll engage with other Engineers in his program, meet some pretty girl with long dark hair and interesting ideas. She'll wear cute glasses and laugh at all his jokes, and his muddy brown eyes will be all on her.

"You mean … I have to leave your condominium?" he

asks, confused.

"No, not if you don't want to. But, like …" I bite my lip, unsure how to proceed.

"You want me to leave?"

"No! I didn't say that." With a sigh, I turn my head, my ear pressed to his chest. "I just meant … I mean, have you thought about it? Do you have a plan?"

His breath dusts the top of my head. It's become noticeably heavier. I don't know if I'm getting somewhere with him, or making everything worse. Likely the latter; I'm so good at that lately.

"I … haven't really thought about it," he confesses, his voice growing quiet. "Maybe a part of me never thought I'd actually get to *be* a student. Maybe I thought I would never earn the chance to prove myself to them …"

"Maybe."

I feel John tense up. His fingers stop moving, as if he's caught in a worry. "Jennifer," he murmurs. "Can you just be upfront with me?"

"How?"

"Tell me what you want." His voice is soft, faraway. "If you want me to move out, I will accept that. I'll … I'll find a way to afford my own place. I should. It might be off-campus, maybe somewhat of a commute, but—"

"Don't be silly," I spit back. "I want you with me."

"Then … Then what do you mean by all of this?"

"I just mean …" Ugh, why can't I just come out and say it? He's holding my hand. He's playing with my fingers. He's held me in his arms every night we've spent in this cruel, dead place. Why am I so certain he'll vanish the moment I utter those three wicked words?

"I think I understand where you're going," he mutters tiredly to my hair. "Ever since we met and you let me stay at your place, what was supposed to be just one night turned into two, then a week … and it almost feels like I still just … happen to be there, almost by accident. Like I don't really belong."

I pull away from him and turn, facing John. His eyes are heavy and his full lips hang open from his words. He watches me, curious why I pulled away.

"I was afraid that you'd leave me when the university accepted you," I tell him, making myself plain. "I was afraid that the only reason you stayed with me was because it was *convenient*. I was afraid, no matter how attached I was growing to you, that you'd one day pick up and leave, and I wouldn't see you in the bed next to me every morning when I wake up to go to class."

"Jennifer …"

"Even the first time we met," I say, all of my feelings choosing this one lovely moment to pour out, "I hardly knew you for more than five minutes before you were tearing off in the other direction, running away from the authorities. Always running away. I was terrified that one day it'd be *me* you're running from."

"I don't ever want to run from you," he says, his deep brown eyes turning to water before me, his lips never fully closing between his sentences. "Why would you think that? You've been so kind to me. No one's ever shown me so much … care. If I didn't feel so damn guilty about it, I'd stay in your condo for good. I love waking up next to you. We work well as a team. We can survive a realm of dangers and bloodsucking nightmares together. There's nothing wrong with … *this*."

He pulls my hand to his chest. I feel the drumming of his heart, its every beat crashing into my palm.

I love that song in his chest.

"If you weren't here with me," I tell him, "I would have lost my mind in that hovercraft. I wouldn't have even made it off the campus. I'd be nose-deep in metal carnage, squished somewhere between the eleventh and twelfth floors of the Histories building."

To that, he leans forward, bringing his face close to mine. "I'm not just here for my own glory." His fingers gently interlock with mine, sending chills up my arms. "I didn't agree to come with you just because I saw my 'way in' to the university, Jennifer. Sure, some part of that motivated me at first, but things are so much bigger now. Bigger, I think, than either of us anticipated. This whole experience here in the Sunless Reach, it's going to change everything. When we get back home—and I guarantee you, we will—I have no plans to give you up, Jennifer, so long as you don't want to give me up. I want you in my life. I want to be in yours."

That's all I needed to hear. Oh, these dumb emotions, making a mess of us worrisome Livings. Using our interlocked hands to pull him toward me, I guide my parched lips to his soft ones. When they meet, a whole lot of fire ignites in the space between us, giving heat to this cold, miserable place. The touch of his strong hands revive me as he rubs my back, pressing me into his body with desire. If we weren't out here in the middle of nowhere, I'm sure that a lot more would happen between us besides kisses of passion and … *hands*.

As John's lips trail down my neck and I turn, shivering with pleasure, my eyes meet Corpsey's, who still dangles. Yes, he's watching. Upon his lazy face, an amused smirk.

"We're not alone," I mutter tiredly.

John looks up distractedly, noting our hanged friend. "So? Let's put on a show, then."

"Let's not."

John chuckles, then meets my lips for one more kiss. After that, I scowl at Corpsey, ruiner of moods, then curl up and bury myself against John's chest, determined to chase a nice dream for a while, escaping the gloom of this world. I take John's sweet suggestion and try to hear my fellow students cheering for me and erupting in applause instead of mocking me. With that sweet hallucination filling my ears, I finally let the exhaustion win.

Somewhere in the dark comfort behind my eyelids, I see my mother sitting in her house all alone. She's staring out the window with a tissue dangling in her hands. Her eyes are dried because she's cried every last tear she could possibly cry. She's processed the news about my dad long ago, only to have it followed with a most grievous call from the university: *"Your daughter has hijacked a hovercraft and flown across the sea. She will never be heard from again."* Not only has my mother lost her husband, but now she's lost her daughter in the very same day. The grief will never end. She ponders her life, glaring at the window.

The next moment, I'm stirred awake by a bug. I swat it away and only succeed in slapping my own face, waking me further. I glance to my left, spot Corpsey still hanging there. I sit up and turn to find John still resting against the tree at my back, his eyes closed and his breathing deep.

Then I feel the buzzing in my pocket. It wasn't a bug I sensed; it's my device. I pull it from my pocket, confused. When I gaze at the screen and discover that a signal has been found and I'm receiving a transmission, every trace of breath is stolen from my chest.

I can't believe it.

In a panic, I mash my finger to the screen, then lift the device to my mouth. "Hello??" I nearly shout into it.

John flips his eyes open, flinching at the sound of my voice. "What is it??" he asks, blinking away whatever little bit of sleep he got.

"Hello??" I shout into my device again, climbing to my feet. "Mom? Is that you? … Mom??" The device sputters, a burst of static exploding from it. The screen shimmers, unable to produce a source of the communication that's somehow miraculously reached it. "Please, talk to me!" I cry into the device. "Speak! This is Jennifer Steel! I'm stranded in the Sunless Reach!"

The thing coughs in my hand, issuing a quiet, whirling squeal for a response. *It's damaged,* I tell myself in horror. *From the river. From low battery. From the polluted air here.*

Yes, that's it: the very *death* in the air is strangling it.

"Mom??" I cry again into the phone, pacing back and forth, tears reaching my eyes. "Help! Please! We're lost! We're going to die out here! PLEASE!"

"Jennifer." John's at my side. "No one's there."

"PLEASE!" I shout at the stupid thing, frustrated that it won't talk back to me. "HELP US!"

"Jennifer …"

I let my frantic stare meet John's. His warm brown eyes ground me, pulling me back into a calmness. When I look back at the device in my palm, there's no light or sound coming out of it. The thing is silent as a stone.

I have a creeping suspicion it was always silent as a stone. *Oh, no. I've gone crazy.*

"I thought I heard ..."

John brings me into his arms, wrapping me tightly against his chest. The device crushed between me and his body, I let the embrace slowly bring me back to reality. *There's no way anyone could contact you from across the ocean,* I remind myself. *You need to keep yourself sane, keep yourself focused. John can't do this alone.*

"I'm sorry," I whisper into his chest. "I'm so dumb."

"No, you're not."

"It's not a convenient time to lose my mind."

"It never is."

"I'm probably just hungry."

"Me too."

"We'll be okay?"

"And so will Mari," he assures me, bringing a hand to the back of my head and petting my hair. "We'll find her. She will be fine. We're not dying out here. Hear their cheers, Jennifer. Their cheers ... Hear them."

"Yeah. Better to hear *that* than a phantom call on my drowned, dead thing," I mumble.

Within the next few minutes, it is determined that we will not find another speck of sleep between either of us. John unbinds the tassel, dropping Corpsey to the ground.

The landing isn't as gentle as I imagine John could've made it; I doubt any love is growing between them. With the pale boy down, we continue on our way through the dusty landscape.

Unlike the area we crashed our hovercraft in, the dead and brambly foliage of this terrain is broken periodically by large expanses of grassless field. The dirt beneath our feet is so dry and hardened, lightning bolt cracks snake across the ground, giving the land a blasted harshness about it.

"How far?" grunts John unkindly to our tour guide.

"The Dead know nothing of distance," he answers cryptically.

John gives a less-than-gentle tug on the leash. "How far?" he repeats, impatiently.

I try a different tack. "You described the Whispers as the place where it all began. What'd you mean by that?"

Corpsey smirks. "It's been called many things. The Great Scar … Death's Aisle … Valley of Shadows …"

"Is it the place where all of the Beau—" I clear my throat, not wanting to hit that sensitive spot again. "Is it the place where all of the *Dead* come from?"

After a moment of consideration, he says, "No one really knows."

"Is that where *you* came from?"

"It was so long ago." A pained expression crosses his

face. "I don't even remember who was first in this world, my sister, or myself. My First Life was so long ago … I struggle to even remember … to even remember …"

"You said only the Dead can go there," I remind him, "to these so-called Whispers. If that's true, how is my friend Mari there?"

"She was taken there by my sister."

I'm trying to piece it together in my head. Through the fog of hunger and exhaustion and plain insanity, it's a very trying effort to make sense of anything at all.

"Wait," interjects John. "Your sister took her? You said before that you'd only seen our friend Mari run away. You said no one followed you across the river, that no one knew you'd come, that no one knew the way to the other side," John goes on, suspicious and irritable.

"My sister caught your friend," murmurs our trusty Corpsey. "She was seconds from draining the woman when I stopped her."

I gape at him. I hadn't realized Marianne was in such immediate peril. These events must have taken place days ago, just after we first fled the hovercraft. This changes everything. "Why'd you stop her?"

"I saw you on that hovercraft. I looked into your eyes and I *saw* you," he says, his voice going quiet and vague. "I told my sister two words … I mentioned that this Mari woman had friends, and among the friends, a special one.

I told my sister two words and she stopped."

"What two words?" I press him.

He smiles at that question, his cloudy eyes turning to the grey, nothing sky, and he says, "Winter … white."

Okay, really. I'm so tired of everyone on this side of the planet making such dramatic reference to my damned hair. My parents are both brunettes, all natural, and both families follow suit. Not a single light-haired among us. Imagine my parents' surprise when I was born. All my life, I've been stared at, told my hair would darken, that it wouldn't stay so … *white*. I was made fun of at school, called albino, diseased, old woman … every sort of silly insult a dumb child can squeeze out of a brain.

"It's just *hair*," I retort back. "Had it since I was born."

"No matter the significance, it stopped my sister." The way he says the word *significance*, it rings so clearly and crisply in his smooth, oddly melodic voice. "She decided right then that she'd keep your friend alive. She sent me to speak to you, to arrange a meeting …"

"That one night in the woods?" I say, confirming it. "You never told me why you'd sought me out! I even *asked* and you never answered."

"The Whispers are near."

Those words draw a cold chill over my bones. John's eyes flash as he looks around, like he's expecting the world to suddenly fold in on itself with some imaginary onslaught of spirits and ghouls and deathly things. None of that happens. We merely stumble through the trees and cracked ground, nothing at all strange or scary or *whispery* in sight.

"Near ..." he murmurs. "Quite near ... I feel it."

The trees quite suddenly give way to a wide expanse of nothing. The ground ahead is flat as a wasteland, grey and dusty. There is nothing before us but an imprecise, swirling mist, much like the mass of cloud in the sky that so greedily keeps the sun and stars from view. It dances and twirls and brushes over the endless wasteland. The sight of which is enough to stop me in my tracks.

The boy looks back at the pair of us. "Isn't this what you wanted?" he asks John and I, and there is no lightness nor amusement to his voice. "I am just as disquieted by them as you are."

I blanch. "By *them*?"

"The Whispers, yes, by *them*," he murmurs, his vague eyes meeting mine. "Do we dare, or do we not dare?"

I look to the left, then to the right. I cannot even see an end. The vast expanse of wasteland is endless in all directions and perfectly flat. Not even a hill or a bump or a stone in sight. The trees at my back suddenly have become a great and generous comfort compared to the utter *nothing* that lies ahead.

"I see nothing," I whisper, afraid. "Where's my friend?

How do I know you're not ... you're not just ... leading us into some horrible foggy trap?"

I can't help my bones from shaking. I'm instantly terrified of this place. There is nothing kind or inviting about it at all. I feel like Dana suddenly, desperate to claim that the spirits are so awful and unrested here, that the spirits are screeching at me from some other plane of existence, haunting me, their eerie voices moaning and groaning in warning, ordering me to turn back, to flee.

"I have not seen my sister in some time," the boy confesses to me, his own voice not seeming at its most comfortable. "We will have to search for a bit."

"Search?" I gape, staring at the swirling mists and the flat, barren landscape. It's like staring into the mouth of Death itself, feeling its cold breath on my face. I have never in my life known terror, not until now. *I don't want to die*, I suddenly find myself thinking.

"Keep me close. I'm your ticket in *and* out of this place," warns the boy, then he extends a hand. "Here, take my hand. We cannot be separated, otherwise you may never again find your way out."

"No way," barks John, not having any of Corpsey's negotiations. "You walk ahead of us, *thing*."

"Afraid? I could hold your hand, too," the boy offers, twisting to get a better look at John despite the noose. "You've a firm grip on that tether, don't you?"

"Don't address me." John's voice is hard, determined not to show any fear. "As soon as we have our friend back, you're nothing. You keep away, you keep those teeth of yours off of us, and you won't know the touch of Jennifer's metal on your face."

"It's okay," I assure John, reaching at once and taking grip of Corpsey's hand. The skin is unsettlingly rough and delicate. I worry any sudden jerk could break his hand off.

A lightness crosses the pale one's face, something akin to amusement, or victory. "Do you even know why we drink blood?"

John and I stare at Corpsey's cocky smirk, waiting.

"It's not for the taste," he goes on, answering his own question. "Or maybe it is, indirectly. See, when the drop of your lifeblood touches my dead little tongue, I get to experience the joy of half-life. I smell the world. I feel the tickle of air upon my suddenly-sensitive skin. If I'm lucky, the generous beams of the furious sun bathe my hungry eyes. *Life*. That's the greatest commodity left in this world and it's through your blood that a sad, Dead thing like me gets to know it once again."

"An experience you will not be afforded on *our* behalf," grunts John in reply, his face tightened with ire. "Move it, Corpsey," he orders, borrowing my placeholder of a name.

The boy, smiling lamely, starts to walk forth. I'm not

yet ready, but I guess I've run out of time whether I like it or not. Hand-in-hand with our Dead companion, I walk alongside him, leaving the comfort of the creepy dead woods and plunging into the unknown. In just a matter of seconds, we are surrounded on all sides by fog. Our field of vision is but a matter of three short paces in all directions, three short paces of perfectly flat nothingness. The swirls of fog waltz around us like misbehaving children. I lose all sense of direction and feel utterly transported to some faraway world with mist for millions of miles in all directions. There is no sign of change anywhere. We walk for five minutes. We walk for ten minutes. In silence, we traverse over a plane that never changes, through mist that never relents, under a white and ghostly sky that never blinks.

"Winter."

I turn, staring at John. "What?"

John stares back, confused. "I didn't say anything."

"Winter white."

I jump, startled by the voice, but find no one standing on my other side. "Did you hear that?" I breathe, feeling my pulse in my ears.

"*... white ... white ... white ...*"

I turn back. The tassel drags loose behind the pale boy. I stop at once. "John?"

The boy turns too. Where once he wore a look of

smugness, even the boy now appears alarmed. "Where did your friend go?"

"JOHN!" I cry out, leaping toward the mist.

The boy won't let go of my hand. "NO!" he shouts. "Don't! You'll be lost! We can't separate!"

"WE ALREADY HAVE!" I scream, thrown instantly into a state of panic. "JOHN! ANSWER ME! JOHN!"

"*Winter …*"

I spin around. I can't even tell which direction we were walking. The mist swirls around us, giving me the uneasy sensation of being in the center of a great, white, slow-motion tornado. The ground lends no helpful hint of footstep or geography. The world spins along with the mist, along with my mind, along with my heart, which is now throbbing in my throat.

"JOHN!" I shout out again, desperate for him to answer me.

He was right there, I tell myself. *Right there!* He should be able to hear my screaming. He can't be more than a few feet away from me. Why can't he hear me?

The haze before me twists oddly, as if bent by some force, the swirling pattern broken for a moment. I wonder if someone is cutting through it when suddenly the mist looks like a face … a really, really big face.

"John?" I ask, all my strength stolen.

Even the pale boy has tightened his grip on my hand

and presses in close to me, fear rattling in his two ghostly eyes. *He's afraid too*, I realize. *This is not his doing.*

The fog writhes in midair again, forming a second face next to the first one. Then a third face. Then a fourth, a fifth, and a sixth.

"What's happening?" I whisper to my only companion left, a Dead boy who's tried to kill me twice, and who's held back from killing me twice.

"I … I …" He can't seem to produce an answer.

Then, from the first face, a figure emerges, parting the mist. It's an old man, naked as his birthday. His skin, grey and silvery like the scales of a fish, is missing in patches, his bright white skeleton showing through, and his eyes glow a furious white, as if his eyeballs were two light bulbs plucked from Marianne's makeup mirror.

Then, to his side, a second figure breaks through the fog. A woman twice as old as him and every bit as naked, her breasts hanging to her belly and her knees bowed inward. Two locks of hair hang in tangled curls straight down to her feet. Her eyes flash as white as the man's.

Two more burst forth: younger men than the white-eyed, so similar in appearance that they could be twins, and they each wear a suit of crudely-fashioned metal armor. Blond of hair and pointy of nose, their eyes glow a sickly, hungry yellow—four bright little suns in the mist.

The final two faces emerge from behind us, giving me

cause to whip around in fright. Both of them are young girls, each dressed in a strange costume that looks like a bunch of rocks sewn together somehow by needle-thin wires, spots of their young flesh visible through it. Their eyes glow the green of emeralds, sparkling and infinite in their facets.

"Who are you?" I whisper, unsure which of the six to address. They have us surrounded, these strange figures, standing on all sides. "What do you want with us?"

The girls with the green eyes giggle, drawing my attention to them, but they say nothing, simply observing me as though I were a curious artifact at a museum, peering at me through the glass. The young armored men turn to one another, their faces scrunched in thought, as if they're linked in the brain and trading thoughts between them. I'm ready to believe *any* sort of explanation for this odd group of guests … magical, scientific, or otherwise.

"So it begins."

I turn to the voice. It was the old naked man, except now his entire lower half has turned into a swirling funnel of smoke, and his hands, now separated, float in the air next to his hips. He seems held together by a breeze. So does his counterpart, the ancient woman, whose legs are now a twisting cone of dust, and her white eyes float in the air on either side of her frail-looking head.

As I'm too scared to speak, Corpsey does it for me.

"So *what* begins?" he asks in his clear, lofty voice.

"To be honest," says one of the young armored men, drawing our attention around to him, "I had thought this iteration would've lasted longer. What a pity."

"Yes, a pity," the other young man agrees, his bright yellow lights-for-eyes flickering twice—which I suspect is indicative of him blinking.

The old man's legs return, the cone of smoke twisting itself into the shape of an amorphous, semitransparent robe, and he steps forward. "You've come to us. So rare in an iteration is it for you to actually see our like."

"So *rare*," the old woman agrees, her voice squeaky and awful to the ear.

"What have you come to us for?" the old man asks.

I blink. Corpsey and I share a look of bafflement. I meet the old man's eyes. "I … I hadn't intended to … to come to you," I admit, at a loss. "I hadn't intended to see any of you. I don't know who … or what … you are. I've only come for … for my friend, Marianne. And I've lost the friend I came with, John. And I … I really would like to go home."

"Home," whispers the woman.

"Home," echoes the young men in their armor.

"Home," the girls with green eyes echo in unison, then look at one another and giggle.

I spin around, overwhelmed with all their voices,

which start to repeat inside my head, spinning around my skull in the form of distant screams and giggling and whispers. Before I realize it, I'm clinging to the side of the pale boy, gripping his hand so tight I hear it crunch. He hardly flinches, too focused on the strange people to care.

"Is this the world that ends in fire?" inquires the old man, and I don't know who among his group he's asking, or if he's addressing the question to me. "Or the one that ends in sacrifice?"

"Or the one that ends in *beauty?*" asks the crone.

"Or the one that ends in oblivion?" asks the armored.

"Ends in war?" asks the yellow-eyed.

"Ends in water?" asks the green-eyed.

"Ends in curiosity?" asks the white-eyed.

"In questions?" asks the yellow.

"In a great big boom?" asks the green.

"In darkness?" asks the white.

"In confusion?"

"In a total standstill?"

"In indecisiveness?"

"In endless, ceaseless cold?"

"STOP!" I cry out, clutching my head with my only free hand, entirely unwilling to let go of the other. "Please," I beg them with my eyes clenched shut, unable to hear another confusing and vague sentence, another annoying rhetorical question, another creepy peep. "Just tell me where my friend is and let me go on my way. Please. I just want to go home."

"You came here to prove the existence of the dead."

I flip my eyes open. The six of them have somehow traded places, or else Corpsey and I have spun around, because the two armored young men now stand before us, their fierce, yellow eyes studying us curiously.

"My dear, you need only lead your people to the body of a dearly deceased," the young man on the left says. "Your father, for example. Surely your people know that living things die, yes?"

"All living things die," agrees the other.

"Yes, obviously," I say, cutting them off, "but I mean to prove to them the existence of the *Living Dead*. You know what I meant." My voice grows stern, tired of their games. "Don't play with me."

"Play?" The armored young men look at one another.

"Play?" The old man and woman tilt their heads.

The mists scream deafeningly as they twist suddenly, twirling so fast I feel my own hair lift from my body. In the next instant, the mist has calmed, the two green-eyed girls standing in front of us now with a strangely amused look on their faces.

"You are the one who plays with *us*," says one girl.

"You've played with us for centuries," says the other.

"It's always you, every time," they say now in perfect

unison, as if they're the same girl and I've just had one too many drinks and am seeing double. "From the moment you're born, we know the end is near. But which end?"

"Which end, indeed?" asks the old man from behind us. "The end of the world? Or the end of the suffering? Why don't you tell us already and stop playing with us?"

"We're so tired," complains the old woman, her voice squeaking like a dog's toy.

I look from the old white-eyed man to the armored young men to the pair of green-eyed girls. "What do you mean 'from the moment you're born'? What do I have to do with anything? I'm just a student at the university."

"A student?" inquires one of the armored yellow.

"Yes," I say, facing him. "I'm a student, and I've come to collect information about my so-named Beautiful Dead with the purpose of proving their existence. I'm going to bring my findings to them, proof of the Living Dead, and make the Histories."

"Oh, dear." The left young man nods, his yellow eyes flashing. "This is the one that ends in arrogance." To that, the armored man on the right groans, saying, "Oh, dear. Arrogance is the *worst*."

"Arrogance?" I ask, disconcerted. "Whose?"

"Make the Histories?" The green-eyed girls giggle. "You're already *in* the Histories! You're in *every* History! So it begins," says one. "So it begins," the other agrees.

I stare down at the girls with the green eyes. Despite the frustration that so quickly invaded my system at the arrival of these riddle-trading glowing-eyed freaks, I find within myself an uncharacteristic calm. In that calm, I discover the whispering and the tittering of the mists to have faded to a nearly indistinguishable hum.

With my hand still gripping Corpsey, I crouch down to bring myself eye-level with the green-eyed girls. "You say I've played with you for centuries?" I ask them.

"Yes," answers the one on the left.

"We knew you'd come," says the other. "You always do. Even if your name is different."

I swallow once, hard. "My name?"

"Vivian."

"Asha."

"Liv."

"Zoe."

"Eve."

"Claire."

"You always come into the world," the girls say in unison, "when it's ready to end."

End. The word sits in my chest like a knife that'd just been thrown. *End.* I catch myself holding my breath, my gaze broken from the creepy green eyes of the girls. *End.* I feel as though I'd been kicked in the stomach.

"If I must be honest," groans one of the young men, "I

am ready for a change. The Living have too long forgiven themselves for their own unforgiveable arrogance."

"Arrogance," agrees the other.

"It ends in arrogance," complains the crone. "What a mess they'll make of it all, the stupid Living."

"The *beautiful* Living," sing the girls.

I turn to the pale boy at my side, searching for a reaction. His sullen eyes say it all: *he believes them.* I can't say if this is just another trick of the realm of the Dead, or if my existence is truly some death omen for the world. That piece of information is so enormous and dramatic that my gut reaction is to dismiss it. How is it possible?

"Do not be saddened by this news," says the old man, his white eyes flaring like the headlights of a car. "Be relieved. The world is like the restless child that won't sleep, and you are its tender lullaby. You are not the *cause* of the world's doom, my dear Winter. You are merely a sign of it … a catalyst, a symbol, a symptom."

I frown. "What did you just call me? Winter?"

"And now that you're here, dear Winter," he goes on as if he didn't hear my protest, "we can go back to sleep, the six of us, and wait for your time to pass so that we may dream of another world."

With that, the crone at his side vanishes in a furious blast of fog, followed by the armored men, whose yellow eyes linger a moment in the mist before vanishing too in a spinning puff of white smoke.

"Wait!" I cry out. "That can't be it! You can't just tell me that because I've been born, the world's to end! And in arrogance, no less! And *horribly!* What the hell am I supposed to do with *those* pearls of wisdom??"

"Make a necklace," suggests the man, and I can't tell if he's being dead serious, or mocking me.

The green-eyed girls flash, dissipating into a funnel of mist, their eyes dancing away until they're out of sight. A swirling dark smoke begins to swallow the one remaining figure: the old man before me.

"Please," I beg him. "Surely something can be done! Can't I take this as a warning? Can't I help the Living fix everything? Can't they … Can't we just … Can't I help *stop* the end of the world? Tell me something!"

The old man smiles, only his face and his blinding white eyes remaining as the smoke swallows the rest of him. "Tell them, 'You did this to yourself.'" Then, in the haze that's left of his face, he finishes, "Tell them, 'The only one left to blame is *you … you … you.*'"

Then the furious winds swallow his face, and as it whips away from sight, the rest of the mists retreat at once, as if blown away by a great wind, leaving Corpsey and I standing in the barren center of a great and endless wasteland, completely rid of the fog from before.

I feel as if I'd just woken from some psychotic dream.

I see the trees from where we'd come in the distance. I stare at them for far too long, lost in the words of the six glowing-eyed figures that still swim in my foggy brain.

"Jennifer!" he shouts.

I turn. John races across the crackled plain, his feet kicking up dust as he approaches. In seconds, he crashes into my body and we embrace tightly, despite my being absorbed in the news of the world's impending doom.

"Where were you?" he breathes, his voice trembling. "You vanished! I called out for you and nothing, there was nothing but whispers and fog and nothing!"

I look up into John's eyes. "You didn't see them?"

"See who??"

"You didn't hear their words? You didn't … You didn't hear what they …?" Already, my questions die on the tip of my sad, Living tongue as my eyes drift to meet those of the Dead boy's, who sadly stare back.

Corpsey and I are the only ones who know. We're the only ones who were meant to hear the message.

But … *why?*

"Jennifer? Who? Who are you talking about?"

Then, as I lift my gaze once more, I see her. Stumbling towards us, a woman with cheeks that still glow like two red orbs of hope.

Chapter Seven

The Doom Girl

"MARI!" I scream, unable to contain myself.

I tear across the wasteland toward my long lost friend, my confidant, my roommate. When I reach her and throw my arms around her, she freezes, too stunned to even hug me back. Embracing her tightly, the tears reach my eyes so fast that I'd think I were somehow squeezing them out of myself.

"I knew I'd find you," I breathe into her ear, choking on my own emotion. "We're going home, sweetheart. I've got you. You're safe."

When I pull away, I find the expression on Mari's pale, bewildered face to be one of utter confusion and terror. *Oh, no. She's traumatized. You did this to her.*

"I'm so sorry," I suddenly find myself saying. "This is all my fault. I should not have let you come. I should have insisted that you stay behind and gone and done this crazy quest all on my own. This was my burden, not yours."

Still, she says nothing, staring at me and trembling,

her purple eyes blank as boards. I notice suddenly that one of her prized purple colors must have fallen out because her left eye is actually black—her natural hue.

"I promise, Mari. We'll get home," I tell her, bringing my face close to hers. "I'll find a way. We will get back to that hovercraft and we will flip that damn thing over and launch back into the sky. I swear it."

Marianne still says nothing, her whole body shaking and her eyes flitting about, as if she worries some great creature is going to pounce on her at any second. *This is all my fault*, I keep saying, even with knowing that she's still alive and finally returned to me, I'm still flooded with guilt—maybe even more so than before.

John's rushed up to our side, the leash still in his grip. "Mari," he says under his breath, then gives her a hug of his own. "We crossed half a Dead world for you."

I smirk. "Now, let's not exaggerate. It was probably just ten or so miles, give or take."

"Give or take," John agrees with a light chuckle, grasping desperately at the excuse for a smile.

Still, there isn't even so much as a trace of a smile on Mari's troubled face. She hasn't even uttered a single word. I turn my eyes to John, wondering if he's thinking the same thing. He meets my gaze and seems to confirm my worries: Mari is haunted-and-a-half.

"Once we're back home," he says quietly, though it's

quite clear that everyone can hear him, "we will all feel a bit less … *traumatized* by our experiences here. We've all been through a lot."

"Yes," I agree halfheartedly, glancing at Marianne and feeling a tinge of disappointment at how unexcited *she* was to see *me*. I'd expected a sigh of relief at the very least, or a return hug, perhaps. Nothing. I got nothing but trembling and nervous staring.

"Run."

I turn to Corpsey, the source of that one, awful word. Then I follow his worried glance to the trees. At first, I see nothing strange at all.

Until the trees start racing towards us.

"THE DEAD!" I shriek. "RUN, RUN, RUN!"

I bolt at once, tearing in the opposite direction, which is *across* the barren wasteland of the Whispers, mercifully sans the annoying sight-hindering fog. John follows, his hand gripping Mari's, who runs along with us, the terror now having grown twofold in her mismatched eyes. Even Corpsey races at our side, though I can't tell if it's due to the noose that's still wrapped around his neck, or if he's actually become bonded to us, running away from his own kind.

I glance back for a peek at our pursuers. Big mistake. There are not just five or ten of them anymore. That damned sister of Corpsey's has amassed a number well over fifty or sixty savage Dead, all of them appearing like a row of black trees that rush across the fogless Whispers in tireless pursuit of us fleshy, bloody fools.

To my shock, another line of trees appears in the far distance where we're headed. To my subsequent relief, these are *actual* trees and not another army of pursuing blood-eaters. *The other end of the Whispers*, I realize as we approach. *We can lose them in those woods*, I convince myself, encouraging my fast-moving feet.

"To the woods!" I shout out, John and Mari trailing behind, Corpsey at my side. "We lost them once, we'll lose them again!"

"There's a town in the woods!" shouts Corpsey. "An abandoned town! You can hide in it! You'll be safe!"

The next instant, we're bursting past the threshold of the woods, scurrying down a path that cuts through the dead, thorny trees. "Hurry!" shouts John from behind. "They're catching up! Hurry, Jennifer!"

The wide-opened gates of the town lie ahead, coming forth to greet me like a friend. My feet carry me under its ancient, yawning archway, narrowly dodging a steel sign that hangs loosely from it.

A sign that reads: Trenton.

"Hurry, hurry!" I cry out behind me, thrusting myself down a thorny, bramble-ridden road that had once been overgrown with vines and greenery, long since died and petrified. Each root and stony tendril threaten to pull at my feet as I stumble over them, my running slowed by the uneven ground. Corpsey leads the way, beckoning me as I race down the winding streets of this long forgotten town, my heart slamming against my ribcage and my feet and legs screaming in agony, fire and acid burning them from within.

Our running comes to a stop when we find the road dead-ending at a brick wall where Corpsey stands. I heave, catching my breath for a second before lifting my chin to our Undead companion and shouting, "Where do we go now?? It's a dead-end!"

John and Mari have come to a rest besides me, too. The three of us stare at Corpsey, whose expression slowly darkens, his face twisting with malice.

"No," I breathe, realizing my error at once. "You lured us here. You … *tricked* us."

His sullen, stark eyes confirm my accusations.

The flooding of footsteps fill the air as the countless Dead race down the street, then slowly come to a stop, forming a Dead blockade of blood-hungry creatures. A disquieting silence falls. Behind us, Corpsey and a great brick wall. Flanking us are the wooden, windowless sides to two buildings. In front of us, a hundred Dead who are hungrily deciding which of the three of us to eat first.

From the crowd of a hundred Dead, the bald sister of

Corpsey takes one challenging step forward, a victorious smirk on her face. That one single ghostly eye of hers squints at us, the creepy, colorless pupil darting hungrily back and forth between John and I, appraising us.

In a fit of foolish bravery, I whip out my device and brandish it, my trusty weapon, its bright light illuminating the dark alley like a great digital torch.

"If you come near us," I threaten, my shaky voice betraying me and deflating all the dumb courage I'm trying to show, "I will *burn* you with my steel!"

The sister, undaunted in the least, takes a few more steps towards us. I turn to threaten Corpsey, only to find that he's circled around us to join his sister, the noose hanging loosely from his neck and dragging along the weed-filled cobblestone. There's but ten paces remaining between us and the wall. Ten paces too few. Ten useless, empty paces.

"I'll do it," I promise Corpsey now, waving my device at him. "I swear it! I'll burn you all and I will feel *no* pity!"

Corpsey comes up to me, slow and quiet as a cat, then reaches fearlessly for my device. For whatever reason, I don't flinch or retreat from him. His fingers wrap around it, then pull the silly, harmless thing from my grip.

He called my bluff. There's nothing steel about it. He likely knew all along.

"Why'd you betray us?" I ask him, defeated.

"I fulfilled my part of the deal," he reasons. "I brought you to the Whispers, and reunited you with your friend." His eyes turn dark, bottomless, and hungry. "You expect me to betray my sister? My sister, with whom I've existed alongside for centuries and centuries? Look," he says with a wave of his hand. "Look at all the Beautiful Dead you've awakened. Coming out of their slumbers. Emerging from their eternal, dark dreams. Aren't we all so … *Beautiful*?"

A stone settles in my stomach. A fist squeezes within my throat, choking out all my dumb, inadequate, Human words. A lightning bolt dances its way down my spine.

"Y-You did this to yourself," I whisper.

The Dead stare at me, all of them turned to stone. John's breath is the only thing I hear. It's the only sound in the whole world.

"The only … The only one left … left to blame …" I start to say.

The sister's expression changes, her one ghostly eye flashing. Her hands drop to her sides, all the fight having left her, and she steps forward, gaping at me with wonder. It's like she's listening suddenly, waiting for my next words, studying me as though I'd suddenly turned into some fascinating, glittering fountain of green gems.

"The only one left to," I go on, "… t-to blame is …"

The sister whispers one word: "Winter?"

I freeze. My eyes gloss over with fear and wonder, as

if all I have left to look forward to is my impending death. My body knows it. My nerves sense it. My heart is racing towards its final, fateful beats. Minutes remain of my life; that's what my body swears it knows.

"Winter?" Her voice is as light and innocent as a little girl's lost in the woods. "W-Winter? Is that—Is that you?"

I shake my head, uncomprehending.

"It's me," she says, bringing a hand to her chest. I swear, if the Dead could cry, tears would be filling her one, ghostly eye. "Winter. Don't you recognize … Don't you … Don't you see …? It's me. M-My brother," she says, a hand moving to Corpsey's shoulder. "You never met. You never had the chance to meet him. He was dead already, but … y-you saved me. Remember? Tell me it's you. Winter, tell me it's you. Please. *Please.*"

Then, another swirling of sound approaches, like a storm, but this storm is not made of twisting fogs and unrested whispering. From above, a great metal bird emerges—four times the size of the one we crashed—its nose casting a light down on our street, toward which all the Dead stare up at, grunting and moaning in protest, shielding their faces from the gusts of wind that pummel down from the bottom of the hovercraft.

"Winter!" cries the bald woman through all of the deafening noise. "Please! It's me! It's *me!!*"

A ramp slides down at our backs, slamming against

the cobblestone. Men and women rush down the ramp with guns aimed, dragging Marianne up, then John, and finally reaching for me.

"Winter!!" cries the sister, rushing forward to catch me, to grab me, to keep me from leaving her. But the guns come between us, and up the ramp I go.

That's when the realization attacks me. "My device!" I shriek, pulling against the authorities who are trying to rescue me. "No!! That's my only proof!! I NEED IT!!" I reach fruitlessly for the brother who took it out of my hands. "GIVE IT BACK!!" I'm furious with myself for letting it go, furious for letting him take it right out of my grip. *I thought I was about to die.* The words ring hollow in my ears. *I thought I was facing the last minutes of my life. I thought I was ... I thought ...*

Then I'm at the top of the ramp as it lifts from the earth, pulling away from the bald sister and her brother who watches me ponderously, a curious, otherworldly expression on his face.

"Tell me it's you!" the sister still cries, even all the way from the ground. "WINTER!" she screams into the sky.

"I'm no Winter," I murmur to her sadly, staring down with a heavy heart. "I'm just the doom girl."

Chapter Eight

Flick Of A Pen

The hum of the hovercraft is all I hear for hours. Wrapped in a soft blanket with a cup of warm tea in my hands, I sit next to John, and across from Marianne and a trembling Connor Easton, the four of us in utter silence as the craft gently carries us over the ocean. Mari wouldn't touch the food they offered us, even refusing the tea, which is her absolute favorite. Still …

"She's my friend," I tell the nurses when they enter our cabin—or should I say *airborne prison cell in the sky*—a sweet-faced boy and a long-faced girl with a hook nose. "She won't eat or drink when she's upset. I know her."

"We need to get fluids into her," reasons the male.

Mari's bewildered eyes meet mine. She wouldn't even let them touch her for a proper medical exam.

"In time," I assure them. "When we get home, I'll …"

It suddenly occurs to me that we may not be headed home. We might be heading straight to the courthouse to be judged for my crimes, or worse. I guess the upside is, we'll be fed in prison, including Mari.

The nurses seem to accept my half-sentence, moving on to East to rebandage the third red eyebrow across his forehead, which has become something more of a cherry-black grimace.

I look up at Connor, struck with a realization at once, and whisper, "Dana?" to which he merely shakes his head and looks away.

That's my last interaction or exchange with anyone for hours. I'm left to interpret what the hell that shake of his head meant. Regardless of Dana's fate, I know one thing for certain: *I've been vindicated.* The crew on this hovercraft saw the Dead with their own eyes, the Dead from which we were fleeing. I may have left my device behind—and all my notes and proof with it—but the crew on this ship know my truth, and they cannot deny it.

The Beautiful Dead *do* exist.

Long after the hot tea's been consumed and all I'm holding are John's hands, I lean my head on his shoulder, closing my eyes for just a moment's rest. That moment's rest turns into a five-hour dreamless slumber.

"Jennifer Steel."

I open my eyes. A tall woman in white-plated armor stands before me, a gun strapped to her belt and a red emblem on her chest. She holds a long gadget, waiting.

"Confirm your identity," she states. "Jennifer Steel."

“That’s me,” I choke, my voice waking up late.

The gadget in her hand glows, a little screen showing the wave output of my own voice, then issues a beep at the woman, who nods in response. I guess I’m confirmed?

Moving on to John, the woman lifts the gadget again. “Confirm your identity.”

“John Mason,” he answers.

The gadget glows. The gadget beeps. The woman moves on.

“C-Connor Easton,” says the boy, his eyes shining with tears for some reason. I can’t tell if he’s happy to be home, or sad. When he lifts his bright eyes to meet mine, I see a sudden flicker of anger in them, taking me aback.

“Confirm your identity.”

Marianne, who still has yet to utter a single damn word since we found her, simply stares at the gadget as if it were the most frightening thing in the world.

“Confirm your identity,” the woman repeats.

“I’m sorry, ma’am?” I interject. “That’s my best friend, Marianne Gable. She’s undergone some serious trauma and hasn’t eaten anything or drank a drop or spoken a single word since—”

“Fine,” says the woman tiredly, putting her gadget away. “Long damn day anyway. Get ready to disembark.” With that, she struts into the main cabin, leaving us alone.

In the peace of our separate cabin, I consider our

mutual silence broken and venture to speak. "East?" I say, my voice soft. "What's wrong? You look angry."

"Can't imagine why," he mutters darkly.

I frown. "We're heading home. We're rescued, East. You'll get to sleep in your own bed tonight. You'll—"

"No, I won't," he retorts. "And neither will you."

I glance at John, who returns my stare with a quizzical one of his own. "What do you mean?" I ask the boy.

"We're all suspects. Criminals. They'll hold us in a cell and question us. My brother shoplifted a bracelet for his girlfriend when I was seven. I know how this goes down. I didn't see him again until my tenth birthday." East scowls at the wall, his arms folded tight against his chest. "My life is ruined."

"You're innocent," I assure him. "We'll all say the same thing. Mari, John, and I will all tell the truth of it. You were simply in the wrong place at the wrong time. You got wrapped up in a plot that—"

"No, I was precisely at the *correct* place at the *correct* time. At my job, doing my duty, just as I should have been. *You're* the one who was in the wrong place at the wrong time. Now, I'll bring shame to my family. My parents will think I'm no better than my brother, no matter the truth of it. They've had three days to ponder why I would've helped assist in the abduction of school property. 'Oh, he's just like Cole,' they'll say. 'He's a thief just like his thief brother.' My life is *ruined*."

I sputter for a moment before saying, "No, East. No, no, no. They won't say that. Your name will be cleared. We'll all make sure of that. East, if it wasn't for you—"

"My name is *Connor*," he declares suddenly.

"I know. But listen to me. If it wasn't for you and your bravery in filling that satchel, we'd all be—"

"Dead as Dana?" he finishes.

I sit back in my seat, the words having pummeled me in the stomach. "She … She's dead?"

"Probably, by now." Noting my confused expression, East sighs irritably and clarifies himself. "When the craft came to the city and found us, Dana told me she'd never return to the land of the Living, not now that she'd found her 'true home'. She went *crazy*, Jennifer." His eyes grow teary and his words bite with accusation. "The woman thought she'd belonged in the land of the Dead all along. She wanted to *stay*. Something's wrong with her. No one in their right mind would choose to live there in that unlivable place. I'll give her a week, tops. She'll die. None of those others will help her, I can guarantee that." East's eyes flood with tears. "She'll go through that s-s-satchel of mine in a day and s-starve until her last *breath*."

With those dark words uttered, Connor Easton shuts up, turning away and allowing his tears of frustration to fall without restraint. Listening to him choke and sputter as the sobs erupt like earthquakes from his chest, I let the conversation rest and lean into John, pained by the boy's words. *I can't believe she wanted to stay,* I think to myself, trying to imagine it. On one hand, it's totally believable. But on the other, how can I not see that as some far-reaching form of prolonged suicide?

I'm the reason for the suffering of everyone in this craft. Even the men and women who came to rescue us. I'm the reason they put their lives in danger, just to save the totally unworthy life of me, and the totally worthy lives of my brave and loyal companions … or rather, my now-eternally-damaged companions.

The disembarking process is smooth and quick. Upon passing down the ramp, escorted by the armed authorities every step of the way, the tired sunlight from a waning evening pours over our faces like warm honey. There is no mistaking it: all four of us pause in our tracks to drink in the light that we've so missed for the past few days. The little bit that shimmered in through the windshield of the hovercraft did not suffice.

As we're brought out of the sun, I realize with a start that it's the president's building into which we're being led. For some reason, I'd expected to be ushered to the disciplinary, if East's fears could be founded. As we walk down the long tiled halls, I see a look of surprise on his face, too; he wasn't expecting a visit with the president of the university herself.

The four of us are seated in a waiting room of sorts, watched over only by two armed men in those clean, white-armored uniforms. I study the pair of them who guard the president's door, curious if they go through a gallon of starch and bleach every laundry day.

The door opens. "John Mason," announces a young man without even looking up from the chrome tablet in his palm, tapping on it and causing it to chirp.

John gives me a look, then squeezes my hand before rising from the bench and moving to the door, which gently closes behind him.

I breathe evenly and stare across the aisle at Mari. She doesn't stare back, her eyes glued to the fluorescent light in the ceiling. I whisper her name and she doesn't react. I hiss it again, trying to get her attention, but poor Mari, she's trapped inside her own head of horrors, and anything I do to get her attention is lost. I lean back on the bench, feet aching, and wait for my name to be called.

Ten minutes later, the door opens. John steps out, but he doesn't return to me. His eyes locked on mine, a guard escorts him down another hall and out of sight. A million words stick in my mouth. Where are they taking him?

The young man stares at his tablet. "Marianne Gable," he announces.

"Excuse me," I say, rising. "My friend's been through

so much that she won't utter a word, not even to me. I don't think she's going to be able to communicate to the president properly. May I go in with—?"

"No," he says, eyes still glued to the tablet. "Marianne Gable."

I look at my friend, who still stares at the light above and doesn't move an inch. "Mari," I say, nudging her with my voice. "They're calling for you, sweetheart. Mari?"

One of the armed men comes up to her side and places a hand gently on her shoulder, coaxing her off the bench and toward the room. Trapped in that eternal daze of hers, she moves. The door closes behind her.

I drop back in my seat. And then there were two. East picks at his nails. I wish I could say something to calm his anger, to make things better between us, to recapture any sort of kindness he might've felt towards me … but every stupid word that crosses my mind is as futile as the last. The only one of us he seemed to connect with was John, whom he looked at as a protector. I stare at East across the aisle, longing for him to show me some sign of care or forgiveness. I'll be staring forever, at this rate.

The door opens. Mari is escorted out at once, still trapped in her daze, and is taken down the other hall, just as John was.

The young man lifts his tablet. "Connor Easton."

Of *course* they'd leave me for last. He rises from his

chair and, like some militant young man, darts straight into the office without a second's hesitation. I experience one single bite of resentment toward him before the door shuts, leaving me all by myself with the two stoic guards.

"I'm so sorry," I whisper to my hands, clasping them and channeling the dead spirit of my dad, the living spirit of my mom back home or wherever she is, all the souls I've disturbed in my fruitless adventure. *"I'm so, so sorry."*

The door opens one final time. East comes out of the room. His whole face is changed. Escorted away, he looks at me with a peculiar softness in his eyes before being taken around the corner. His changed demeanor startles me. I don't know what to make of it.

"Jennifer Steel."

With a stone in my throat, I rise from the bench, my weight supported by two annoyingly wobbly knees, and make my way to the door. The president's office is a grandiose one, filled from one end to the other with antique furniture, mahogany bookcases, and the scent of summertime. The far wall is made of glass from floor to ceiling, much like my condo, and a desk that's four times the span of one sits stretched before it. One fateful chair rests in front of the president's desk.

"Jennifer," says President Vale, standing on the other side of the aforementioned long-as-hell desk. "Come."

I cross the office and put myself in the chair, which is

outrageously comfortable. I've never met the president up close, but she is every bit as beautiful as I've heard. Her freckled skin is velvety and fair as cream. Her hair, wavy and ruby-red, drapes down to her shoulders, and her forty-something round face, plain and featureless, is warm and welcoming. President Vale wears a green pantsuit with a white scarf tied loosely around her neck, and two emeralds dangle from her ears.

"President," I say quietly, acknowledging her.

"We have a lot to discuss."

I opt to keep my words to myself, not daring to speak until I know how much the others told her, until I know the punishment I'm to face, until I know how soon I can begin divulging all that I've seen, and justify my crimes.

"You, Jennifer Steel, and your friends, John Mason and Marianne Gable, along with the involuntary and, as I'm made to understand it, unintended company of both Connor Easton and a woman by the name of Dana, last name unknown, did willfully steal a university hovercraft and travel overseas to the Blight with the purpose of proving the existence of the Mythological Undead of yore. Do I have the facts correct, Jennifer?"

Her voice is so gentle that the words seem to carry no hint of accusation or admonishment. I can't say there's a single thing in her statement that I can contradict.

"Yes, President," I answer.

"Please, call me Rosella." She clasps her pale hands together, the nails painted ruby-red as her hair. "I will list a few more facts that I would like you to either confirm, or deny. Will you do that for me, Jennifer?"

I nod. "Y-Yes, Rosella."

"Good." She smiles amicably. "Is it true that you, in fact, *did* encounter the Mythological Undead?"

"Yes," I confirm.

"Is it true that the previously mentioned woman by the name of Dana chose, of her own free will, to *remain* in the Blight?"

I'm suspecting "Blight" is their scientific name for the Sunless Reach. Having been there and walked its scorched terrain, I will not contest that most fitting name. "I did not witness her voluntary decision to stay. I only heard of it through East. Uh, sorry." I cough. "Through Connor."

"Very good. You're doing well, Jennifer. Thank you for your cooperation." President Vale offers me a smile, then tilts her head, her waves of red hair bouncing. "Finally, is it true that the university-issued device—upon which you took notes and gathered evidence of the Mythological Undead—was left behind in the Blight?"

"I'll pay for it," I insist, my voice quavering.

"Just answer the question," she urges me politely.

"Yes, Rosella," I confirm. "True. Yes."

"Very good." The president, appearing oddly relieved,

offers me a genial smile. "I welcome you, Jennifer, back to Skymark University. You are so, *so* very lucky to be here. Your life is important to us, and we will do whatever we can within our power to help you return to normalcy after your … unfortunate experience. We, here at the Skymark University, extend—"

"Wait a minute," I interrupt, despite my own promise to myself to shut the hell up. "You're not charging me with the crime of stealing the hovercraft?"

President Vale smiles again, her lips pushing the cherries of her fast-reddening cheeks so high, her eyes vanish for a moment. "Jennifer, you have been through much in the past three and a half days. I think you are due for some time allotted to reacclimate."

"Reacclimate," I mutter, unsatisfied. I almost *want* the charges, as mad as her calm demeanor is suddenly making me. "That's it? And are we just going to gloss over the fact that I … that the *four* of us … just uncovered the greatest lie of our time?" I ask, jamming a finger down on the desk as if to drive my point home. "My Beautiful Dead exist. The subject of my studies. The stuff of legends, which you so politely refer to as *Mythological Undead*. Here's some news for you and the rest of the world: there's nothing mythological about them. They're real. They're on the other side of that ocean. And they *bite*."

The president nods, the smile on her face wavering

but a bit, the way a flame wiggles at the attack of a sudden breeze. "I had wished to give you some days to recover before addressing the handling of your experience. If it is your wish to address that now, I will be more than willing, provided that—"

"Handling?"

President Vale pulls out her chair, gracefully lowers herself into it, then leans across the desk with her cherry lips pursed and her eyes, bright. "Skymark is not going to pursue any criminal charges. But … there is a condition."

"A condition," I say flatly, waiting for it.

She nods at a paper and pen that rest on the desk in front of me. I look down at them, confused.

"You must sign a statement," the president tells me, "that says you have been to the other side of the world, and found *no* sign of the Undead."

Her words are the crack of lightning that lights a night sky. I hold my breath, gaping, and wait for the rumble of thunder to reach me.

"In this statement that rests before you," she goes on, "you will claim that Dana the Diviner, a known fanatic of the spiritual and the metaphysical—as well as a mentally-unstable individual—kidnapped the four of you and took you with her to the Blight."

There it is. "What?!" I rasp, outraged. "We can't—!"

"You will deny seeing anything over there but decay,

ruin, and nothing," President Vale explains. "You will—"

"I will not!" I say, rising at once. The chair falls back with a loud thump against the tiled floor, sending an echo through the room. "Why would you deny this?" I ask. "I've been to Hell and back, quite literally, with the sole purpose of proving the very thing you're telling me to deny to the world! This is big news! This is something *everyone* should know! This is … This is *groundbreaking!*"

The president, unfazed by my outburst, lifts her chin and studies my fury with sympathetic, doughy eyes. "Jennifer, if it wasn't for your impetus and thirst for knowledge, none of your friends' lives would have been put in danger. I think my offer is reasonable."

The blame game. The guilt game. I happen to be an expert at these things, and the president cannot outplay me. "And you'll rob me—*a student with impetus and thirst for knowledge*—the opportunity to make the Histories and prove, once and for all, that the Beautiful Dead exist? Can't you think about what that sort of discovery would do for Skymark? For the whole school? The world will be at our feet! The sponsors … The media … Why are we shutting this up and acting like it didn't happen??"

"There are powers greater than I, Jennifer. I'm just a woman, like you, a woman who happens to run Skymark University. But there are powers greater, powers that run the city, powers that run the government, powers and powers and *more* powers above me. I'm but one voice in a sea of far more powerful voices, Jennifer, and my options are limited."

I stare at her, my resolve crumbling at the thought. Is she saying that the government knows about this too? Am I kidding myself with this grand dream of mine?

"Without signing this statement," sweet President Vale continues, "the university will be forced to take action against you. John, Marianne, and yourself will be charged and convicted of your crimes—as you've just a moment ago confessed to them—and after a very quick trial, you'll be imprisoned for the remainder of your lives. Not only for stealing the hovercraft," she goes on, "but for the reckless endangerment of students' lives, including the unwilling innocent, Connor Easton. The story we've spun about Dana will become a tale of *you* abducting *her*," she adds, "and without her here, she could easily be presumed dead. We're talking a potential murder charge, Jennifer. Once that's in the hands of the court, neither I nor the university can protect you. They'll deem you crazy. You'll be sent to an asylum for *adjustment therapy*. Do you see how vulnerable you become without this statement?"

I stare down at the paper, stricken by the realization of the dangerous corner I'm being painted into. Is she really protecting me, or is she protecting something else? Something … darker?

"President—*Rosella*," I say, correcting myself. "I had even considered, beforehand, coming to you directly to ask to overturn my professor's order. He told me to omit the Undead from my dissertation. But, for years, I've—"

"He was following orders," says the president. "Same as I. This statement protects his best interests, too."

I shut my mouth, silenced utterly by her words.

"Professor Praun was asked to hold an audience with you regarding your studies," she explains calmly. "He is only doing what he's been asked to do, Jennifer. There is a reason we keep those tomes in the Mythologies library. No one has ever taken the subject into such a light, trying to prove the stories as fact—until you."

"Praun ... But, he ... he was ..." I'm at a total loss.

"Jennifer." The president reaches forward suddenly and takes my hand, giving it a squeeze and hanging on as she speaks. "I was just like you at your age. Oh, how I pushed and fought for my place in this world. I don't want you to lose that fight in you, Jennifer. Don't let this experience discourage you from your dreams."

"Why can't they know?" I ask quietly, tears finding my eyes. "Why must it all ... Why must it all go to waste?"

"This is bigger than you and I. Even the crew that rescued you, they keep the secret too. It *must* be kept. An ocean separates us from them, and for a good reason." She takes my hand into both of hers now, squeezing, the urgency of this matter being made clear through her pleading eyes. "My sweet Jennifer. I urge you to sign the statement. This is the only way to exonerate you of your crimes. Your mother will be so happy to see you again."

"My mother," I say, hit at once by the notion that *her* fate rests on whether my signature is on that paper, too.

"I didn't even tell you the ways in which all of your friends will benefit from your signing this statement," the president goes on, her eyes gleaming. "Connor Easton will return to his post as a delivery boy, should he want to. Your friend Marianne, she will be given as much time as she needs to recover before returning to her classes. And John Mason," she adds lastly, a knowing shimmer in her eyes, "will be accepted as an official student here at Skymark University, starting next term."

That last sentence breaks my knees. I balance myself with my free hand on the desk. John will get what he wants. Marianne will have time to heal. Connor will not follow in the criminal footsteps of his brother. And I …

And I …

"And I get nothing," I whisper.

"Don't be silly, Jennifer. You'll be officially pardoned for your … *misjudgment*, we'll call it. You'll be treated as a survivor, Jennifer. A survivor of a very traumatic and grievous occurrence at the hands of a "divining" lunatic. You will be able to return to your lessons without any interruption," explains the president. "Your dissertation is in two days. I'll even allow you another week of time to prepare, should you need it. You'll only be asked to revise your section on the so-named *Beautiful Dead* to agree with the statement set here before you. Professor Praun will be exceptionally proud of you, Jennifer, and your peers will welcome you back as a survivor … a hero."

"And all of my wrongs," I add, "will be blamed on Dana, an innocent individual."

"With all due respect to the Diviner, she is a world away, and will suffer no consequence. It is the right thing to do, Jennifer. You're releasing all responsible parties with but a flick of a pen. Please." The president squints at me with urgent emotion, her lips pursing as if she wished to kiss me. "Sign the statement."

I stare at the cruel paper, not really seeing it, not really seeing much of anything. Then, staring at the paper, the worst of it all stabs me right in the heart.

"The others already signed their own statements," I whisper, realizing the truth of it the moment the words touch my lips.

The president nods. "All we need is yours. Then your lives will continue as they did before. Your fate's in your own hands, Jennifer Steel." She offers me a smile, and a gentle nod. "All you need to do is sign."

With a signature, I will make the Dead truly die. With

one little flick of a pen, I will thrust the Beautiful Dead into Mythologies, into fiction, into the silly fluff of nightmares and children's storybooks.

The truth will have to live and die in my heart, my beating, raging heart … where it always was, and where it always belonged, I suppose.

With a quivering sigh and a million regrets in my fingertips, I pick up the pen and stare once more at the statement. *Winter.* I feel the twirl of mist around me, the memory of the six rushing forth. *Winter, don't. Please.* I see Truce. I see the Mayor. I see Corpsey, all these faces I'm about to sign out of existence. *You did this to yourself.* I see his bald, one-eyed sister begging for me to recognize her, crying for me, reaching. *The only one left to blame is …*

I bring the pen to the paper.

Chapter Nine

Dissertation

Two Living days later finds me standing by the glass wall of my condominium, watching as the sunrise paints the world in gold. It's the day of my dissertation. I ache all over. Everything's so far away and numb and *lively*. Ugh.

"Ready to go?"

I turn to John, my totally legal and allowed-to-be-here roommate. He's dressed in a form-fitting button shirt and jeans, his hair styled handsomely and his eyes sparkling with excitement. He didn't do anything about that stubble on his face, but I'll let it slide; you can't take all the rugged out of John.

"Not really," I confess.

He comes across the room, his boots knocking heavily on the floor. "Still raw about the denying-the-Dead bit?"

"No." I hug my dissertation to my chest, its contents bound into a metal-jacketed book with steel wiring along the spine. I insisted on steel. I demanded it at the printers, ignoring the looks my odd request earned me. "It's Mari."

He glances at the closed door to her room. She hasn't come out of there since we came back home. What a lovely so-called "recovery period" she's having in there. The therapist that visits has yet to get Mari to utter one damn word. Oh, how damn helpful everyone is.

"She's going to need time," mutters John, but I hear the uncertainty in his voice, too. Just like I heard it in the therapist's. Just like I saw it in the pretty, hollow eyes of President Vale. Just like I saw it in my mother's eyes when she visited me earlier this week. Yes, we had a good cry. No, I didn't miss my dad's funeral. They've rescheduled on account of my being gone, as well as my dad's wishes to be cremated. No, I don't wish to describe the meeting with my grief-stricken mother in any form; my heart is plenty heavy enough for the time being, thank you.

"So many unanswered questions," he murmurs, lost in thoughts of his own, I suppose.

"And we'll never have them answered, John. We all signed the agreement." As if I have to remind him. "Might as well forget that any of it ever happened."

"*She'll* never forget," he mutters. "Who knows if she'll even honor the statement? If she even knew what she was signing? The moment she starts speaking again, she'll spill the secret to the world and doom us all."

"No." I shake my head, refusing to believe it. "The old Marianne will come back. She just …"

"… needs her time?" offers John with a smirk.

I pull John towards me for a hug that I desperately need and enjoy the feel of his firm body against mine, but it does less to calm my nerves than I'd hoped. Our hearts beat heavily between us, two drums in a band. Well, right now it's more like a heavy metal band.

"What about … the *other* people who were there?" I whisper over his shoulder, worried.

"The less-than-friendly alive ones in After's Hold? I don't know, Jen. We may never know."

"They got over there somehow."

"I don't know." He kisses the top of my head, running his hand up and down my back. "We have to let it go."

"I know."

"Maybe we need time, too."

I pull away and bring my mouth to John's. I'll never get tired of how our lips feel when they touch, and what silly things it does to my pulse. "Can I meet you outside?"

"Of course," he agrees, then gives me one dashing smile before leaving the condo.

I bring myself to Mari's door. After taking one deep, long breath, I put my knuckles to the wood. "Mari," I murmur quietly. "Can you hear me? Mari?" There's no answer. Surprise. "I'm coming in, Mari."

The door creaks as it opens. Perched on her bed, just as she has been for the last few days, Marianne sits in a sea of bed sheets and uneaten food. The room smells of something fettered and something else foul—the food she's refusing to eat, I suspect. Not to mention that she hasn't even had a damn shower since we've been back. No concern for hygiene, no concern for health ... I had to *beg* them not to take her to the hospital. I insisted that time home was all she needed. It's bound to be any day now that the therapist will decide Mari needs a stronger treatment, then whisk her away to some hospital far away from here and from everyone she knows.

Caring to spare my friend's feelings, I make every effort not to cover my nose and mouth when I address her. "I'm just checking in on you, sweetheart."

Mari's eyes meet mine. She still says nothing, not even bothering with the lifting of a hand or the shifting of a foot. She's been planted in that exact position for days. I wonder if she's even slept properly.

"I'm really worried about you," I tell her, my heart breaking the longer I stay in here. Or maybe that's my nose breaking as I stifle every gag and choke that my body is trying to make. "Can you, at the very least, come out of your room so we can talk?"

Her odd, mismatched eyes stare at me, wordless.

"My dissertation is in an hour. You know, the one in which I have to deny the existence of the Beautiful Dead. Wow. Isn't it such a sad thing? The world we live in? Here we went, thinking we were taking some adventure of a lifetime, only to be robbed of its treasures the moment we return." I sigh heavily, suddenly carrying a conversation with myself. "I know, it doesn't help to talk about it. I should be really careful … not that it matters anyway. We have nothing, Mari. We don't have a lucky zombie foot. We don't have some magical amulet. We don't have a device full of wisdom, nor one damn photo."

I clench shut my eyes. All of the events that took place in the Sunless Reach race by my eyes like some wild dream I had. Did it even happen? Was I actually over there in the wretched place of my darkest dreams? I don't even dream about them. When I sleep, the only things I dream about is chocolate pudding and imaginary places in which I'm having fun and making a fool of myself. Only when I wake does the dark and heavy reality return to me. Strange, how I thought I'd be more traumatized by the experience. Instead, I almost …

I almost miss it.

"This is just stupid," I say suddenly. "Mari, I'm taking you out of this room. You're going to come and witness my dissertation," I decide, marching up to her bed. Yes, the stench grows exponentially as I approach. "You have been hearing me go on and on and on about it all year. I won't let you miss the great and gloriously *anticlimactic* payoff. Yes," I say, answering the strange and questioning look on her face, "it will be as boring as you fear."

When the door opens and John turns, his eyes flash with surprise when he finds Mari at my side. "Oh," he grunts, his eyes turning suspicious. "Is she okay, or …?"

"No," I answer for her, "but I'm not going to let her miss my dumb dissertation. Mari's my best friend, and I want her with me because I love her."

I give my offensively stinky friend a squeeze, to which she reacts by staring at me like I'm the Horror From Hell. Maybe I am.

"Everyone's going to be there," John tells me, almost like a warning. "The whole school, probably. Everyone wants to hear what you're going to say about—"

"About that *thing* I gotta deny," I finish for him. "Let's get it over with. I'm *so* ready to bore everyone to death."

Then, across the breezy campus we go, the morning sun washing over us with unapologetic life and fervor. Every step draws me closer to my destiny. This pathway that I've strolled a thousand times from the condos to the Histories building, this is *my* Broken Road of Destiny. The way has always been a broken one, the path cutting left, cutting right, then deceiving me as I push through the mazy woods of life, but I know that at the end of the path rests a light, a furious green light, and I will not give up until that satisfaction is in my warm, Human palm.

Then I'm in the auditorium standing before the entire

student body of Skymark University, and all that strength and brave-crap stuff I just talked about is gone.

"H-Hello. My name is Jennifer Steel," I state timidly, my voice projected through the sound system to the six or seven thousand students that have woken up early this morning to hear me, "and this is my dissertation on the Histories of Northern Mythos, the Fall of the Old World, and the Rise … of the Beautiful Dead."

Word spread. Not a soul on campus wanted to miss this. Even the entire Engineering school came, taking up a section in the back. President Rosella Vale herself sits near the front with a committee of esteemed colleagues. I'll pretend she's here to appreciate my hard work and not just to ensure I abide by my sworn statement. Right in front of her sits Professor Praun, focused like a hawk.

And so I begin my dissertation. The crowd is so large and the lights are so bright that I can't even spot John in the crowd, nor Mari, who's seated next to him. Every word that I offer to the vague shadows is lapped up in perfect, thick, and respectful silence. Never have I ever felt my words be more attended to. I could trick myself into believing that they're truly interested in my studies on how the mythologies of ancient northern civilizations influenced and gave birth to our way of life today, or how the greed and obliviousness of our ancestors led to their sudden and unfortunate downfall, but the truth is, they are, each of them, just biding their time until I reach the true heart of my dissertation … a heart that no longer beats … a heart I'll be forced to deny is there at all … a heart called the Beautiful Dead.

"The Rise of the Beautiful Dead," I state, reading the title of the final section of my work.

Instantly, the energy in the room changes. People shift in their seats, leaning forward to hear my precious words of gold. Oh, if only I commanded this much importance in all areas of my life.

"I have long thirsted for the truth behind the Beautiful Dead," I tell the thousands upon thousands of pairs of eyes that excitedly watch. "My mother read the stories to me as a child, and my imagination was forever changed. My father, who recently … who recently passed away, did not have any love for the subject. Many don't. Many feel that it is a wasted study, or a superfluous study, or not even a study at all. Some say it's just some gross and highly unsubstantiated exaggeration of ancient sciences that once claimed to grant immortality, to cure all disease, to reanimate the dead. The answer to the one disease that we all share, the one disease that no man, woman, or child is immune from: the disease of being alive. Its inevitable result: death."

Death. The word flitters across the room like a stray needle of black smoke, threading itself through the crowds of countless ears and hungry brains, coiling up and down the aisles of this enormous auditorium, staining the world with its undeathly memories.

"The answer has had many names: The Fountain of Youth. The Elixir of Life. The Tree of Ages. The Eternity Pill. The Crimson Candle. The Infinity Glass. Anima ..."

Anima.

I close my notebook; I won't be needing it anymore. I take one deep breath. The world waits patiently for me to gravely disappoint it.

"I recently went on ... an adventure," I tell them, no longer reading my notes. I speak from my heart, and from a vow that bears my signature on a paper somewhere. "It was against my will, though a part of me was quite thrilled to go, despite the circumstance. A woman named Dana kidnapped me and my friends to a place that is only described in those storybooks of my childhood. A place that we all fear is where we go when we pass. A place I thought my father could be. A place beyond the sun's reach, where the Dead live and the Living die."

The room could not be more silent. Never will the world know a room filled with nearly ten thousand silent and completely attentive bodies. Not a breath is drawn. Not a finger twitches. Not a foot shuffles, nor a cough issues, nor a paper crinkles. Vast, pure, heavy silence.

"It is with great disappointment and ..." I shiver, my

nerves betraying me, my legs feeling weak. "It is with great, great disappointment that I report ... that there was nothing ..." I'm gripping the edges of the podium before which I stand, upon which my closed steel notebook rests. My knuckles bleed white. "Nothing at all," I press on, my teeth grinding one another, "that would support, validate, or prove ... the existence of the Beautiful Dead."

There is a shuffle of feet. Then a sigh. Then a hundred sighs and a hundred shuffles of feet. "Come on," grunts someone in the front. Then a thousand. "LIAR!" shouts a girl. "FAKE!" from a deep-voiced man somewhere else.

I'm in the Whispers again and the voices are circling my head, taunting me, mocking me, threatening me.

"It was my hope to find proof of the Mythological Undead," I go on, trying my best to drown out the shouts of outrage that steadily grow among the crowd, "but I was regrettably unsuccessful. The only thing I found over there was decay, ruin, and nothing. I—"

"YOU'RE A LIAR!" someone else cries out.

"Attention-seeking bitch!"

The shuffling of people getting up to leave become staggering, like a herd of beasts crossing the wild, except these ones hurl insults as they go. I beg them to hear me out, to sit back down, to listen to my final conclusion, but I can't even hear my own voice through the uproar.

Then, a young woman emerges from the crowd,

stepping down from the seating area and crossing the front of the room toward the stage. Her act causes the room to quiet, if just for a moment, curious of her plans. Maybe she's going to attack me, just like half the room likely wants to do themselves. Maybe she will wring my neck on behalf of the whole student body.

I stare at her, those cheeks still glowing a faint, dulled red. "Mari?" I question. "W-What're you doing?"

She faces the room, her mismatched eyes curious and wide. The room watches her, all the shouting having died out, leaving an eerie and unsettled tension in its wake. At any moment, the bomb of anger could go off once more.

"Mari?" I prod her, genuinely worried.

Then, my friend utters her first words since we've been home: "The Beautiful Dead *do* exist."

No one responds. No one stirs. The crowd has turned into a tableau of students, half standing, half still sitting, all of their eyes glued to the likes of Marianne Gable.

"Mari," I say, my voice dancing across the room. "You don't know what you're saying. You've been through a lot. You're just—"

"And I can prove it," she announces to the room, ignoring me.

My mouth opens and closes and opens again, unable to produce a word. What the hell is she doing?

"M-Mari …" I repeat, half a whimper.

It's just her word against the world's, I decide at once, no matter what silly thing she's about to say to the room. *She is trying to stand up for me, but everyone knows she lost her mind,* I tell myself. *They will take her to a mental hospital. The statement we all signed will still stand strong. Marianne will be dismissed as crazy, and nothing more.*

Then Marianne, my best friend in the whole world, draws an object from her pocket, showing it to the room. "This is a knife!" she states excitedly, the sound system picking up her voice and throwing it at the crowd, whose expressions are now a thousand shades of terror.

I stare at the knife, the stage lights shimmering off the shiny, serrated edge. "M-Mari. Put down the—"

"The Dead are alive!" she exclaims.

Then she stabs herself in the head.

I don't know which I hear first: the screams of horror that explode from the crowd, or my own.

As quickly as the screams came, they're gone, replaced by a hum of the thickest, tautest silence I've ever known. The world watches Mari as she stands before them, a blade buried into her head, and a smile on her proud, red-cheeked face.

"I don't even bleed!" she says proudly, the echoes of her words bouncing around the room. "Look at this! I can take it out, too!" She does so with some minor difficulty. Each time she tugs on the knife, her whole head goes with it. "I think it's stuck," she complains, half to herself. Then, after a two-handed yank and a horrible squishing sound, the knife slips out, taking a clump of her hair with it. "There we go!" Then, as her strange eyes focus on the crowd, she asks, "Still not convinced? Need a hand? It just so happens, I have one too many!"

With that, she swings the knife onto her other wrist in an effort to chop it off. The knife gets embedded instead, stopped at the bone with a sickening *thump*. The audience wheezes and gasps, repulsed. A man faints in the front, collapsing into the woman at his side. A scream that could wake the dead bursts from elsewhere in the audience.

"I'm proof!" she shouts, hacking at her hand. "Me!"

Dodging her erratic movements, I manage to get ahold of Mari and tug on her, determined to get her off of the stage. "Mari," I beg her, desperate, "please, Mari, stop, don't do that, *stop*, Mari!"

"I'm the proof of the Beautiful Dead!" she cries out, happy as a sunflower. "It doesn't even hurt! I swear!"

"Mari!"

Security officers have cautiously approached the stage armed with an array of guns, and I back away at once, my hands in the air. Mari, the moment she sees them, giggles suddenly, then says, "Ooh! Can you give me a hand with my hand, officers? The knife is stuck, as you can see …"

Two men come forward, each taking one of her arms,

and then they less-than-gently usher her off the stage and toward a side door exit, where she vanishes from sight in a giggle, still chatting with them like it's just another Friday. The audience hums with scandal and horror.

Trembling, I slam myself into the podium for one last appeal. "Don't believe what you've just seen!" I cry out. "It was all an act! It was fake! An illusion! A toy knife!"

But more security guards come to take me too, and amidst the buzzing of the crowd, I'm dragged towards the same side door. Behind me, I hear the voice of Professor Praun flooding the auditorium to demand order, making assurances to the room and threatening disciplinary action to anyone who persists in acting unruly.

Just before being pulled through the doors, I catch sight of President Rosella Vale, but from this far distance, I can't measure the expression on her face. I don't know if she's exuding the calmness she so afforded me when there was nothing but a desk and an unsigned paper between us, or if there's threats and deadly promises now in those sweet, well-meaning eyes.

Chapter Ten

I Will See You Again

"I think I have amnesia," she murmurs to me quietly, "because I don't really know things that I should. You and John and Willa—that's my therapist—have been kind to me. Have we known each other for long, you and I?"

"Very," I agree tiredly, sitting in the chair beside her and trembling. My stomach fell out from under me hours ago. No one's spoken to us. Not Praun. Not Rosella. We have no company, save the four walls of this small room.

My life is over.

"I wasn't entirely sure at first," admits Mari, suddenly the most talkative person in the world, "but at one point, when I was by myself in that bedroom, I started to piece together a few details. For one, I realized it had been a whole day and I hadn't needed to eat. That struck me as particularly odd," she goes on, her face wrinkling, "and then I realized that I didn't … well, you know."

"Humor me," I mutter, miserable.

"I didn't have to *pee*," she says, whispering the last

word. "No bodily functions. I thought it was so bizarre, that I hadn't noticed until then. Finally, I had a wild idea and … and I put a hand to my chest. I listened and I … well, I sat there on that bed and listened for my heartbeat for two whole days. Spoiler alert: I still haven't heard it."

My head is a chaotic swirl of conflicting thoughts and what-if's and brain-wracking. I keep wanting to deny that I was ever in the Sunless Reach. Listen to me, already believing my own lie that has my signature next to it in the president's office.

Marianne, my friend, my *changed* friend … She is the same person, and yet she is a complete stranger. The Mari I brought to the realm of the Dead is not the Mari I brought back. Is it even safe to say she changed? Or is it more accurate to say … that she *died*?

She died. Those words cut me so much deeper than even the grotesque sight of a knife through her head does. *She died over there, and the magic of that realm brought her back … except different.*

"Why are you shaking your head?" she asks.

I look at her. I want to cry suddenly, looking at her innocent expression and her one-purple-one-black eyes.

"I shouldn't have done it," she says suddenly. "I know. It was a mistake. I got you in big trouble, didn't I? I was just sitting there listening to all of these strange people attacking you. I realized what you were saying and … and seeing as you're my only friend in this world, I needed to protect you. I'm so sorry."

"Don't apologize." My mind is a tornado of questions and worries. "I'm the one who should be sorry. I'm the reason that you're … you're …"

I can't even say it. I'm not even sure I believe it yet, even after her performance. I'd verify her *lack* of a heartbeat myself, if I wasn't so terrified of having that very truth confirmed.

So instead of confirming any of that, I simply study Marianne's face, searching for that best friend and roomie of mine deep inside her, then dare to bring a hand up to her soft cheek. I feel her flesh, curious if I might notice any difference in it. She watches me with her big sweet eyes. The red on her cheeks still glow so faintly, you would almost think they were just naturally that way, a symptom of her abundant joy. A symptom …

What if my birth really *does* signify the beginning of the end of the world? If I believe that nonsense, then what if my silence about the Dead is securing that end? What if, instead of being a symptom of the end of the world, I'm merely a sign of a *change* in the world?

What if defying that silence is the key to saving all of humanity? What if it's my *duty* to reveal the truth?

"Will I ever remember my life?" she asks me, like I'm the expert. "Or is it gone forever?"

Suddenly, I realize I *am* the expert. I've been to the realm and back. I *am* the expert of the Dead, no matter if I'm allowed to admit their existence or not.

"It's called a Waking Dream," I murmur, channeling the book-buried face of the ever-tall Mayor Damnation. *Damn you for having such a ridiculous name, Damn it.* "You'll have it quite suddenly, I'm told. You won't know when, but at some point, all the memories of your First Life will jump right back into that sweet head of yours." I offer her a tentative smile. "Think of it like a memory pill."

"Ooh. I hate pills. Ooh!" she realizes with an excited jump. "I never have to take any ever again!"

"Marianne," I say to her, trying to reel in all the focus and seriousness that I can. "You remember the statement you were made to sign? You remember what it said?" Her big eyes lock onto mine and she nods, her glowing cheeks jiggling. "Alright. It's very important that we *stick* to that statement, should the president or any of her people come to talk to us. Not only *our* wellbeing is at stake, but also that of John's, and our delivery friend Connor. What you did in the auditorium was an illusion, okay? An act. Fake."

"Illusion. Act. Fake." Mari frowns. "Mistake."

"That's right," I encourage her, putting a hand on her shoulder. "Stick to that, and everything will be just f—"

The moment I utter the words, the door opens to reveal the stern-faced, eyebrow-free Professor Praun. His presence casts a coldness through the little room I bet even *Mari* can feel. He takes one step inside, then shuts the door behind him and leans against it. His eyes, the whites of which flash with intensity, observe the pair of us for way too long. I want to crawl out of my skin and surrender myself to the army of savage blood-eaters just to avoid another second of his silent ire.

Then, he says, "Good save, Ms. Steel."

My face wrinkles in confusion. "W-What?"

"The 'It was all an act!' bit." His face turns pensive as he studies me. "Might've saved all of your lives, in fact. Once order was restored in my hall and the students were dismissed to their respective colleges in an organized fashion, it was determined that the majority of them did, in fact, believe your friend's act to have been just that: an act. One last, desperate little act—done by Jennifer's best friend and roommate, no less—to get people to believe in your ridiculous claim about the Dead Who Live." He lifts a brow at me. "Am I made clear, Ms. Steel? It was an act, and nothing more. The last two people we must convince of that is the pair of you."

I nod quickly. "It was an act. All an act. Right, Mari?"

"Illusion. Act. Fake," she repeats, as before. "Mistake."

Praun studies her with a hardened expression, as if weighing the sincerity of her claim. Then he nods once curtly, as if satisfied, and turns his attention back to me.

"With your dissertation behind us, the president has granted you a week's leave from campus, Jennifer Steel, so that you may have time to sort your affairs with the passing of your father … as well as other things."

The news comes as a shock. "But I have some math exams! And … And I have a reading assignment, as well as an essay due for my Archaic Languages class, and—"

"All of it will be taken care of," he assures me blithely, though his face never smiles. "You need your time, Ms. Steel, whether you want to take it or not. As Marianne doesn't have much of a family to speak of, she'll—"

"I don't?" Mari looks at me, confused. "I … I don't?"

"She'll be going with you," finishes the professor, "and you *will* be monitored. Consider your actions and the antics of your 'well-meaning' friends, Jennifer. Remember the statements you signed," he says, his eyes narrowing, which always sits so oddly on his face, what with the eyebrows missing. "It would be a shame for anyone else to disappear much in the same way that your 'abductor' Dana did. Am I made perfectly clear?"

My teeth clatter within my skull. I'm out of options; *that* much is clear. "Yes," I say quietly.

He turns then and opens the door, intending to leave.

I rise, swelling with a passion that I can't ignore any longer. "You knew about it the whole time." I'm ripe with the curiosity of years of research and *yearning* that I will soon be made to shelve permanently. "Professor, please. Tell me why you didn't stop me sooner, why you let me learn so much, only to silence me when I find the answers I've been seeking. You owe me that, at the very least."

He stops in the doorway, his head turned halfway in my direction. He wears a smirk of amusement, the closest thing I'll ever get to a smile from the cold and stoic Praun.

"Oh, how I've always admired your hunger." He turns a bit more to meet my eyes. "May you always be hungry, and never know the true emptiness of death."

The door is left open when he departs, leaving Mari and I in a quiet soup of mystery and wonder.

"Today is the first day of the rest of your Second Life," I tell my friend days later, after she's all packed for our weeklong trip to my home. I had to help her pick through her things for hours, seeing as she had no idea what she owned. "You ready to go on an adventure?"

The light returns to my roommate's eyes, which had been somewhat lacking the past few days. Mari, the *real* Mari, she's still in there somewhere. I'll coax her out a little bit each day. But until she's fully back—and until she's had that Waking Dream that the fuzzy-haired Mayor Damn went on about—I'll take the little flicker of light in her eyes to be all the answer I need.

John doesn't start classes until the next term, which gives him the perfect excuse to come with us too. He has nothing to fill his days with but time and research, so I borrowed six different books from the Skymark Library on Engineering for him. He's read three pages so far. "I'm more of a *hands-on* kind of guy," he explained to me when I teased him about how little he'd read, and that innuendo of his turned into a tease that ended with our clothes on the floor. It was a very nice day.

"I'll meet you by the shuttle!" exclaims Mari, carrying her bag outside and letting the door shut behind her.

John comes out of our room right then and sets his heavy bag on the couch. Then his deep, rich eyes run up and down my figure, as if seeing me for the first time.

"You look nice," he tells me in that gruff, barbaric way of his, bringing his stubbly face to mine for a kiss. It feels more like a bite with all the aggression he puts into it.

I pull away with a chuckle, just to get a good look at his face. Our adventure has brought us so much closer together. Something's built between us that I'm not sure was there before. A bridge of trust, maybe. We depended on one another in that dangerous realm—you know, the one that totally doesn't have walking dead things in it.

And maybe one day, he'll say he loves me. And maybe he never will. Maybe he'll never need to, always showing it in his own rough, brooding, John-like way.

"Your heart's racing," he observes, our bodies pressed against one another. "Am I doing that to you?"

"No," I assure him. "It's just a strange sort of awful symptom of being alive. I think you're afflicted with this most troublesome condition, too. See?" I put a hand to his chest, my palm enjoying John's strong, healthy pulse.

He clasps my hand, a twisty smirk finding his lip—that signature *John* sort of smile. "I think it's just a symptom of being near each other."

"Then we better prepare for our hearts to race a lot."

"Every day," he breathes as his lips rush to meet mine.

I want to say this trip is going to heal us. I want to believe that I'm not really a symptom of the end of the world. I want to think that we can truly put the Beautiful Dead behind us, that it's all over with.

But I fear it's only just begun.

Epilogue

The Whispers are silent today, and the Winter girl's totally-not-made-of-steel device flickers in my bony hands, its last breath of life shuddering within it. It must be alive, this strange artifact, because I'm witnessing it die before my eyes.

I've been touching its face, learning the ways of its inner workings. I made its face change several times. It's an odd little thing, this metal creature that belonged to Winter, to Jennifer, to whatever her name is and was. The face became an image of a man in a beige suit. The face became an array of words I couldn't understand. It turned into many things before my eyes, just with the swipe of my long, bony finger … this odd, chrome chameleon.

My sister took off with the rest of the Dead that she gathered. So heartbroken at the Jenny-Winter woman's departure, she didn't even have the heart to face me. Poor sister. She will hunt for the blood until the end of time.

I push my finger at the chrome chameleon, and then it

plays its worst trick of all. Its face turns into hers. Upon its flickering, dying face, it shows Jennifer and her beautiful white hair. Completely unmoving, the image of Jennifer stares at me, her eyes sharp as icicles. I bring the face closer to mine, mesmerized by it. All around her, the shimmer of colors that play in most candles kisses my eyes. What a wonderful and terrible thing to do to me, this evil chrome chameleon … to torture me with its last breath.

Then, it turns to darkness. The little metal creature dies. No life left. It didn't even bleed. Does it have any? I bite at the thing, chewing its corner. I gnaw and I chomp, unsuccessful in puncturing its hard, metal skin.

No life left.

Nothing.

Until the end of time.

I walk the Whispers for as long as my legs will take me. The mists never again greet me, and I'm certain they never will. The Whispers care so little for us Dead. They bring us here, the mists and the hisses and the screams, but they abandon us too. Humans are so foolish at times, feeling they've nothing to live for. What I wouldn't give for a taste of that life again … that life I can't remember.

How cruel, to have had my Waking Dream so long ago that I can't even remember what I'd … remembered.

It's then that I see the blemish in the endless waste of

the Whispers. A mysterious thing that catches my eye. I move quicker now, rushing to meet the strange anomaly that I have found in the Whispers.

I drop to my knees, hearing the cracking of my bones. I pluck the curious treasure off the ground, examining it in my gritty, grey palm.

It is a shining, emerald-green stone that now rests in my hand. A gift from the Whispers, I suppose. A message to the Dead. A challenge, perhaps …

And to that pretty green stone, I offer a faint smile and one little word—whispered, of course: "*Anima.*"

To Be Continued …

Did you enjoy *The Whispers?*

Turn the page to read the COMPLETE PROLOGUE of the next book in the Beautiful Dead saga: *Winter's Doom.*

Prologue

Anima.

I know the word. My sister knows the word. The Dead hiss and whisper and grunt upon the uttering of that vile, strange, beautiful word.

Yet here I sit, a glowing green stone in my palm, full of the theoretical stuff of Undeath, and I don't know how to use it.

Do I speak to it?

"Awaken," I growl, but my word is lost to the dead trees, the mist over my head, and the dark.

"Come to life," I command it, but the proud, green thing only stares back at me.

"Anima!" I demand tiredly.

Nothing and nothing.

When my sister comes through the trees to find me—her feet snapping the lifeless twigs, tiny bones, and dead things beneath them with every footfall—I always tuck my pretty treasure away at once. I don't know why, but I feel a great and terrible possessiveness over it, like I can't stand for the stone to be in anyone else's hands. I must protect it with my life.

Well, with my Unlife.

My Undeath.

My *whatever-one-might-call-it.*

Every time my sister comes by, she looks upon me with her one eye and her one empty eye socket, and she asks the same question: "Any sign of Winter?"

Winter.

My sister hasn't used her own name in a century, yet she remembers at once the name of the woman with the winter white hair.

Despite her name being *Jennifer*, my sister insists on the name *Winter* for the Living girl who came and left.

And when I give my inevitable grunt of *no*, my sister makes the same scowl, then murders her way through the deathly woods, muttering and grunting to herself as she picks irritably at the one or two hairs left on her otherwise bald head, disappearing.

And I'm left alone again with the green stone.

And my thoughts of *her*.

Winter. Jennifer. Whoever she is.

I close my eyes and hold the stone to my chest. I find myself wondering what my sister knew of that woman.

I've done this many times since Jennifer left this land

on that giant metal bird in the sky, that creation of the Living, that thing that makes loud noises and cuts across the sky. Countless times I've held this stone, struggling to remember a thing I never knew.

Behind my eyelids, I see something for the first time—a camp.

My eyes flash open.

The dark woods surround me again.

What was that vision? What was that place?

I grip the stone tighter and clench shut my eyes once more, desperate to return there. And at once, the camp bursts to life before my closed eyes. I feel young, small, youthful. Am I a child? Did I die as a child?

I feel my sister's grip on my hand, tight and strict and protective—as protective as my own hold on this green stone right now—as we stroll together through the camp.

Where is this place? What is it?

The memory tries to fade, but I hold on with every ounce of me, desperate to see it to the end.

And at once, my real feet pick me up off the ground and I'm running through the dark woods with my eyes still closed, chasing the dream as if it was real, as if I was running toward the very camp itself. The brush is all unfamiliar—dead trees and crunchy grass and gritty air—yet the scent is eerily the same.

It's a deadly scent.

A nothing scent—all that the Dead can smell with their lack of the sense of smell.

At once, I feel the trees open around me. I'm in a clearing, yet my eyes remain closed. I inhale deeply, desperate to smell something, as if the memory itself gives off a scent I might track.

I see an army of Dead storming that camp. I hear the shrieks and cries of Living men, women, and children. A woman hides. A man hurls himself into a tent. Two children run into the woods, screaming.

One of the men stands against the Dead with a giant hammer in his hand.

John? Is that John, the man who came with Jennifer to this place?

Before I can have any opinion of it, my sister—my Living, two-eyed, full-haired sister—turns to me and cries out, "Run!"

I'm a slave to the memory, running the way my child self did, tearing into the woods with abandon. It isn't long before I realize my sister is no longer running with me, having fallen behind to protect the camp. I'm alone.

I call out my sister's name. No one calls back.

Then the child that is me looks up into the sky, terror in his heart—in *my* heart.

And with my Living eyes, I see the sun.

I've almost forgotten what it looks like. It isn't the

eternal grey swirl of nothingness that us Dead see. No, with Living eyes, I see a beaming blue sky broken only by the reaching web of branches overhead, and a bright yellow circle of sunlight pouring over me.

Then the jaws of a Dead person whose name I'll never know find my face before I can even scream.

I jerk away from the memory, the green stone falling to the stony ground at my feet. I shake with terror as I back against a nearby tree, paralyzed with fear.

It was like a second Waking Dream, remembering at once what took me from that world to this one.

I peer up into the sky. It is only grey again.

Grey and dead as I am.

Was it due to the green stone that my memory of that day became so vivid? Was that stone responsible?

I snatch it right up from the forest floor, then stare into its depths once more.

And it's while peering into those depths, dark curiosity burning in my unbeating heart, that I see it for the first time, something new, something strange.

A face.

And in that green, glowing Anima, that face stares curiously right back at me.

The Beautiful Dead saga continues with

"Winter's Doom"

Made in the USA
Columbia, SC
25 June 2024

37536010R00124